HELL

AND

HIGH

WATER

SUMMONER FOR HIRE
BOOK TWO

Domino Finn

Published by Blood & Treasure, Los Angeles
First Edition

Cover by James T. Egan of Bookfly Design LLC.

Print ISBN: 978-1-946-00842-8

DominoFinn.com

Demons are Real

Not only that, they're everywhere. Shadows, secrets, strangers. Dark beings with mythic powers every bit as dangerous as their legends.

Opening your eyes to this reality isn't easy. Devils are crafty. Supernaturals hide in plain sight. Even wizards will do anything for power.

What you need is a professional. Someone with nothing left to lose. A tour guide to Hell who packs enough smarts and resolve to navigate anything in your way.

What you need is Shyla Crowe, a smooth operator on a very bumpy ride.

Welcome to the thrilling world of *Summoner For Hire*. It may not be virtuous, but it's a living.

Previously in Summoner For Hire

The biggest burden in life is family. Don't let anyone tell you different.

I thought I was in hock to a demon, but the truth is so much worse. Abaddon, the Angel of the Abyss - he's the one that owns my marker. And if I don't play nice he kills my father.

He's too powerful. I have no chance of taking him on. Not even my hellion familiars can get me out of this jam. Abaddon holds the Ring of Solomon, making him a more powerful summoner than I am.

But I'm a daughter of Solomon, and that ring is my birthright. Unfortunately, the demon jailing my father wants it too.

Asmodeus has a personal grudge. He was once a slave to the very same ring so entwined to my ancestors, and now me.

See what I mean about family being a burden? Only my problems are just getting started.

Which brings us to now...

HELL
&
HIGH WATER

SUMMONER FOR HIRE
BOOK TWO

The Marker

I held the mic hidden in my sleeve to my mouth. "Eyes on the package."

The underground dance club was alive with frenetic activity and sound, straining communication through earpieces. The crowd bounced to the irregular rhythm of music best described as witch house: slowed down hip hop beats remixed into something sensual, layered with kick drums and garbled vocal samples. It was a surreal backdrop that complicated a simple job. At least the atmosphere allowed our team to operate covertly.

We were in a lounge area walled off from the main dance floor. Red vinyl booths lined two walls and a bar lined the third, with loose tables and chairs in between. My vantage was on the fourth wall halfway up a metal staircase. It gave me a bird's-eye view of the VIP table where Ray, the owner of the establishment, sat.

He was an interesting character. A provocateur with too much money and not enough to do with it. His sales pitch for the place was that it wasn't an ordinary dance club. It was a playground for spellcasters, summoners, and worse. His club was a neutral ground for things that otherwise didn't belong in this world. With solid connections and the right password, you too could join the outlaw underground.

Like most marketing pushes, it was a case of over promising and under delivering. There were magicians here, sure, but they were dime-store practitioners and occult hobbyists. And while it wasn't beyond the realm of possibility that there might be a vampire hiding somewhere in the crowd, the vast majority of guests were knockoffs in Halloween drag.

But at least Ray had a sense of humor about it. The club was named the Puzzle Box. It was just the right amount of campy 80s nostalgia to make the place work.

"I have it on the feed," said the Wire through my earpiece. As our tech guy, he was holed up in the back of a van across the street, overseeing the job through the club's own low-light cameras. If there was a way to exploit a security system, the Wire knew it.

"Give it a sec," I said, pushing into the metal banister as a couple brushed past me upstairs. The attractive girl wore yellow contacts, though it was hard to tell for sure with the colorful lights. A furred foxtail hung from the back of her miniskirt.

I turned my attention back to the table. Ray sat at its head, three women to his right and his main squeeze on his left. A diplomatic messenger sat across them in the round booth. The man, in keeping with the theme of the Puzzle

Box, wasn't a man at all. He was a silvan from the Low Elemental Plane.

More importantly, he was the client.

Rounding out the table's occupants, the Lead sat beside him. She was the face of our deals, and the team overheard the exchange through her microphone.

"It doesn't look like much," stammered the silvan. His briefcase of payment looked much more substantial than the item he wished to purchase.

Ray was a debauched man with a gold suit and high hair. He dramatically flashed his teeth. "Looks, my fellow intruder, are ever deceiving. That guise you wear, those clothes, these are the things of glamour. This stone comes from the foundation of Maqad itself." He twirled the geometric diamond on the table. It was bulky but compact enough to comfortably hug in a fist, and it was the color of a fading sun. "Do you know how difficult it is to pluck matter from the Aether?"

The Lead eased the tension with a falsetto chuckle. "I'm sure it's perfect." She placed her fingers around the package and everybody smiled.

My eyes brushed across the spacious room to a large Hawaiian propped against the bar. At one point he'd played offensive line on the losing end of a championship game, but that was a different life. "Okay, Heavy," I signaled. "Move in."

The Lead's sharp intake of breath came through the earpiece. Ray had clamped her wrist before she could pocket the stone.

"Not so fast, beautiful." He blinked pleasantly while the Lead's arm strained against his tight grip. "That marker is one of a kind."

"Shit," announced the Wire. "The deal's going south."

"On it," barked the Heavy. His pace to the table quickened.

I clenched my jaw. It wasn't smart to get into it with Ray. Not on his turf.

"Payment was already negotiated," admonished the silvan at the table.

My boots clanked on the metal steps as I descended, ready to take action if needed. But I keyed in on Ray. His eyes were alight, his smile hungry, but he was eased against the cushions, one hand still in his woman's lap. No one else in the crowd was headed for the table.

The club owner wasn't making a move, he was negotiating.

"Wait," I called over the air. "The Lead can handle it."

Her eyes flicked my way as if cursing me, but it was a momentary lapse. If anyone could control their outward emotions, it was the actress. The Lead.

She cleared her throat. "Now Ray, I was told you were a man of your word."

His grip on her arm loosened slightly. "As I am. But I know nothing of you, so let me be explicit. The marker's mine. Your payment garners fifteen minutes of its use, after which it must be returned to me."

"We're here to buy, not rent."

"Then you misunderstand the terms. But there they are,"

laid bare before the transaction. I'll even be charitable by allowing you to back out. After all," he said with a simper, "I wouldn't want to spoil my generous reputation."

The silvan brooded. I didn't know who he wanted to contact or what his diplomatic message consisted of, but I knew it was important. That was the secret part of our job, direct from the Custodian himself: discover the contents of the message.

And apparently that message was more important than the payment and the marker. The silvan grunted in agreement. "I accept your terms."

Ray grinned and released the Lead. She pulled the package away and massaged her wrist. I met the Heavy's gaze and nodded. We were a go.

The offensive lineman stopped at the foot of the table, two bodyguards in his path. They stared at him eye to eye, which was notable because they stood on an elevated step and he didn't. Still, in a place like this, you couldn't count on size alone determining the big dog. We were, as a group, only human.

"He's okay," said Ray, brusquely waving his guards aside. "My, you are a big one."

The silvan and the Lead slid from the booth and joined the Heavy.

"Remember," warned the club owner, "the marker is mine. Return it or you'll owe more than just money."

The Lead winked. "Be right back."

The Heavy parted the crowd and the others followed, making their way toward me. I scanned the tables and dancing revelers in their path. Exotic humanoids pressed close in sensual embraces, rubbing, kissing, lost in the music. Many had pointed ears. A shirtless man had curled ram horns over his ears attached in the back by a leather strap. A stray eye or two caught the large Hawaiian, but everybody was more interested in their own good time.

"Keep an eye out," I warned the team, searching ahead of them. "Ray is just the type of swindler to steal his own treasure to put us in his debt."

The Lead pocketed the summoning marker and pressed into the Heavy's back. They were halfway across the room without incident. Satisfied the way was clear, I headed down the stairs.

"Giving up overwatch," I reported. "Keep an eye out for anyone sketchy."

The Wire laughed over the radio. "You're in the Puzzle Box. Everybody around is sketchy... Wait."

I paused on the last step, eyeing the perimeter. "What is it? What do you see?"

His voice came back measured. "There's a large Pacific Islander headed your way. He looks like bad business."

"Damn right," chuckled the Heavy.

My lip crooked but it didn't do any good for my nerves. "Very funny, Wire. How's my hallway looking?"

I turned toward a receded doorway in the wall. It was attended by a bouncer, but passage through had been prearranged. I nodded and he nodded back.

"Very quiet and very lonely," answered the Wire. "Just the way you like it."

I ignored the dig. The others joined me at the door and the bouncer opened it. The Lead placed the rock in my hand.

"Come with me," I told the silvan.

We stepped into the brightly lit corridor and the door closed behind us. The silvan jumped as we were cut off from the rest of the team.

"They're keeping watch outside," I explained, which didn't seem to comfort him. Until now, the Lead had been with the client every step of the way.

"Who are you?" he asked.

"More than a pretty face." From the sealed hallway, the music was a muffled drone of synthetic drums. "I'm the Handler." I held up the summoning marker. "The only one who knows what to do with this little guy."

"Let's make it quick then. This place gives me the creeps."

That was funny coming from a silvan, a bona fide member of the fae if there ever was one. They lived in an underworld of dark tunnels and twisted creatures. It made me wonder what my client's true form was, but this profession thrived on anonymity. Just another wrinkle in my plan.

I led him into a dimly lit storage room. Boxes of soda syrup and bar supplies were stacked against the walls. A circle of ash was already prepped on the tile floor. "Get the door." I kneeled and placed the summoning marker in the center of the pentagram. "You're a diplomatic messenger?" I asked offhandedly.

He locked the door. "Something like that."

"For who?"

"Better to leave that part out."

I shrugged like I wasn't interested. The silvan had hired us as a bridge, to get the Low Elemental Plane in touch with the High. It didn't mean he wanted to share.

"Here goes nothing," I said.

Summoning was often about ritual, about making sure everything was perfectly in place and that you were perfectly protected. I was an old hand at this, my preparations had already been done, and contacting an elemental was child's play. I waved my hand over the circle and the summoning marker twitched. The rock was a conduit to a specific person or group, someone normally insulated from people like me. That made them special.

The rock twitched on the floor, then tumbled and turned like a die. An airy form oozed up from the pentagram. Like sludgy yet sentient swamp water, a faceless protrusion turned to me.

I stood and backed away, but not too far. "Relay your message."

The silvan dropped to his knees. I craned my neck, checking over his shoulder to catch any whispers or signals. I didn't know why my boss wanted this information, but it was why I was here. The silvan's money would pay our expenses and fund future operations, but his information was the real windfall.

"Tell him it's time," said the silvan.

His voice wasn't especially guarded, but the clipped

sentence was all he said. He pulled a rolled parchment from his waist and held it over the circle. The bulbous slime within extended. As soon as it contacted the scroll, it sucked the paper within its translucent body. And then, as if ten years passed in a moment, the paper disintegrated, its essence being absorbed by the strange fluid.

"It will be done," came a withered answer.

Damn, the use of a parchment meant no audible message would be exchanged. These guys didn't even trust their own summoner, which meant they were serious about security. Still, I had a harness on the elemental. I could get the info after dismissing the client.

The silvan snatched the marker from the circle and poured a pouch of sand over the pentagram, promptly dismissing the messenger and severing my connection.

I pulled the silvan away and shook off the uncomfortable disconnect. "What the hell was that?"

"We don't want any snoops."

I grunted. "Don't mess with my work like that. You could've set the thing loose." I rubbed my boot over the circle, dusting away the evidence.

And then I had a weird feeling like maybe that had been the silvan's intention. The elemental *was* loose. The wispy thing was free to travel anywhere in the steppes now. It could be delivering its message to anybody. I eyed the walls suspiciously. Nothing but boxes and shadow. A memory of glowing amber eyes made my hair stand on end.

"Let's get out of here," I said, disgruntled.

He got the door. The brightness was welcome, as well as

the emptiness of the hall. The silvan went ahead as I cast a last glance inside the storage room. There was nothing in there. I shut the door and followed as the client re-entered the club. As the door opened, music exploded through the corridor like a physical force.

I paused, swearing I'd heard something. When I looked behind, there was nothing. With the music blaring again, it was impossible to be sure.

The Lead's sharp scream spun me around again. The bouncer flew backward through the doorway, hit the interior wall, and collapsed on the floor. The Lead dashed into the hall and passed me, running from something.

"Bernard!" I called.

With the scent of sulfur, a stone gargoyle appeared at my side. We charged past the downed bouncer and into the club. Bernard's bat-like face and wings drew some attention from the crowd.

"I lost him," hissed the Heavy. He clutched his bloody pony tail and pushed to his feet.

I scoured the crowd and reported into the microphone. "The client has the package."

"The dance floor," called the Wire.

Bernard and I surged past the tables and into the larger adjoining space. Two performers dressed like devils paraded around on stilts. A woman in a bikini hung upside down on a long tail of scarlet cloth hanging from the ceiling. Drums kicked into high gear and the dance floor strobed with multi-colored lights. A figure pushed through the center.

"Take that side."

My hellion went one way and I ran around the other. The crowd was thick but the outskirts presented few obstacles. An incidental shove or two made quick work of the pursuit. Whoever we were chasing had a kidnapped silvan in tow.

"Back door," reported the Wire. "After the bathrooms."

"I see it."

The gargoyle converged before I did. He bashed the locked door open and I sprinted in. It was another access hallway, though not as well lit. We scrambled through to another door, pressed inside, and skidded to a stop.

The silvan and his attacker were both unconscious on the floor. A man wearing a white tank top, jeans, and red cowboy boots stood over them, waiting casually with his arms crossed.

Unfortunately, I knew exactly who he was.

"You've been ignoring my calls," said Cisco gruffly.

I cursed my life.

The Outlaw

Rarely was I at a loss for words or action, but I stood flabbergasted at this new development.

"No," I stressed, "I don't want anything to do with you."

"Watch out," he warned. "You're gonna hurt my feelings."

Cisco Suarez was well-built and ruggedly handsome, but he was also trouble. A necromancer and shadow charmer out of Miami, he was both hardheaded and capable. It was a dangerous combination. I had a run-in with him a while back, and if I never saw him again it would be too soon.

Bernard emitted a low growl and strategically paced to his flank. Cisco spread his arms to ready a counterattack.

"Call off your dog," he spat.

"Or what?" challenged Bernard. "The way I remember it, you weren't too hard to put down."

Cisco's face darkened unnaturally. "Your problem being, I always get back up."

"Hold on," I said with a clipped breath. I pulled my stun

gun from my jacket just in case.

Cisco arched an eyebrow. "What is that?"

"Just a little insurance."

"If you say so."

The last time we'd met, Cisco was the mark. More specifically, I was hired to catch him. Between Bernard and me, we actually managed to get him in irons, which helped nullify his magic, but it didn't stick. Animists like him were full of tricks. I knew spellcraft but I couldn't tease matter the way he could. In the end, it was only another group of wizards that had saved the job.

"Where are you?" said the Wire over the air. "I don't have you on a feed."

I put my sleeve to my mouth. "We're okay. Give me a sec."

Cisco waited without surprise as I communicated with my team. He'd likely been watching us. He knew there was more than me and he wasn't concerned one bit. The truth was, I didn't think the others could help.

"You're poison," I told him. "Everything you touch goes to hell. The media's all over you."

He shrugged. "Sensationalized pulp."

"What are you doing here?"

"Funny. I was about to ask you the same question."

The man on the floor groaned and, for the first time, I got a look at the silvan's attacker. His skin was powdery white and his bald head had numerous black studs that resembled bone formations, looking like an albino Darth Maul. He groggily raised his head.

Cisco held up a finger. "Hold that thought." Then he lifted his boot and dropped the heel onto the thing's head, knocking him out cold. "Now where were we?"

Bernard was still in a defensive stance. That was natural for him—gargoyles loved to pose. I was already working out what had happened. The attacker, likely under orders from Ray, had attempted to abscond with the silvan and the marker. It was Cisco that had foiled his escape.

"You weren't following me," I intuited.

"Following you? No. I'm in town because of you. I've been calling you, repeatedly. For a week. But why I'm right here, right now?" Cisco nodded toward the silvan, who was slowly regaining consciousness himself. "I was after this guy."

"Why?"

"He's one of the king's trusted messengers. You know, Vesuvius himself. He has a line on something I'm working."

I arched an eyebrow. "You know the king of the silvan kingdom?"

"Hey, don't lump me in with that double-crossing asshole. I wouldn't say we're friends or anything." He took an authoritative step closer. "But it is disappointing to see him working with you."

Bernard growled in warning. They faced off, but I only laughed. They both turned to me, off guard.

"He hired my team to deliver a message to an elemental." I pursed my lips. "Wait a minute. Do you know the contents of the message?"

He snorted. "That's why I'm here."

I grinned in amusement. "Me too."

Cisco studied me, gauging the truth of my words, but he seemed to operate more on instinct than careful deliberation. It only took a second for him to shrug it off and turn to the silvan on the floor. Using the toe of his boot, he rolled the messenger to his back. Just like that the animist had his back to the summoner and her familiar. He no longer considered us a threat.

Digging through the silvan's pockets until finding the summoning marker, I spoke into the microphone. "Package is recovered. Set up in the hallway and keep watch. I only need a minute."

I was still mulling over how I would turn this situation to my advantage and get the information I wanted. Cisco was more direct about it. He put his boot on the silvan's chest.

"This is what's gonna happen," he announced. "You're gonna tell me what was in that silvan dispatch of yours, and if I decide I believe you, I'll let you live."

Ugh. That was one way to ruin my professional reputation. My client gave me a startled gaze. I looked up at Cisco and he flashed me a wink, like we were kids in grade school and he was about to take some poor sap's lunch money.

"You can't do that," protested the silvan. "I'm under her protection."

"And look where that got you."

The netherling huffed irately and pushed to his elbows. I recoiled as twines of shadow rose from the floor and wrapped around him several times, squeezing his arms to his side and slamming him back to the floor. Cisco had barely wiggled his fingers.

"Hey," snapped the shadow charmer, "I want you to focus. In fact, fix your eyes on that stone demon over there. Look into his ugly bat mug. Closely inspect those snarling teeth. Don't think he wouldn't be happy nibbling on your leg."

The gargoyle hiked a shoulder. "That sounds delectable, actually."

"Bernard," I chided.

"I'm serious," said Cisco. "There's only one way you're getting out of here in one piece."

"It's for the convocation, all right?" The silvan panted against the constricting shadow magic. "After the wedding, King Vesuvius is announcing the expansion of his family."

I frowned. "What wedding?"

"His daughter's," explained Cisco. "Good kid. I was there. That can't be what this is about." The twines tightened.

"I swear!" hurried the silvan under immense strain. "It's what always happens when there are major changes to the ruling families."

"And who's on the receiving end of this message?"

"I don't know."

Cisco's eyes narrowed and the black shadow tightened.

"They didn't tell me!" he cried. "I passed on the message. The elemental is taking it from there."

"He smells scared," noted Bernard. "I believe he's telling the truth."

"You can't be serious."

"He is," I said. "And I think he's right." I tugged at the silvan's chest but stopped short of touching the black magic. "Loosen those things, will you?"

Cisco grumbled and let up a little.

"Okay," I soothed, nodding encouragingly at my client. "I'll get you out of here, but you need to tell him what he wants to know. When and where is this convocation taking place?"

He almost objected, but one glance at Cisco changed his mind. "Saturday night, eight o'clock, at the Conway House. That's all I know."

"The Conway House?"

"You know it?" asked Cisco.

"Yeah, it's the mansion of a local philanthropic organization. What do they have to do with the Elemental Planes?"

"Sounds like the perfect cover to me." Cisco leaned close to the quivering silvan and grinned. "A deal's a deal." The shadow twines dissolved and my client breathed deeply in relief. "Now, remember, don't tell anyone that you told us. I won't kill you, but if your king finds out you betrayed him, he will."

I helped him up, feeling a little bad for the guy. He was my client. Cisco's methods were a little rough, but I couldn't deny he'd come through.

The silvan brushed off his shoulders and quivered when he gazed at the knocked out creature beside him. "What is that thing?"

"You mean you don't know?" asked Cisco. "I figured it was a Nether fiend of some sort."

"I'm not so sure," I cut in. I bent down to check the horn nubs and was surprised to find they weren't fake. "This isn't a Halloween costume like some of the others."

The gargoyle sniffed at the unconscious figure. "I hate to say it," he grumbled, "but they smell like they're from my neighborhood."

The silvan scowled. "Ray has hellions on his payroll? Is that what he is?"

"I don't know what he is," I said. "In my world, it's not outside the realm of possibility."

Cisco prodded the hellion with his boot. "Whatever he is, this guy wasn't hard to put down. Let's hope Ray only sent his B team."

"Where's the marker?" asked the silvan.

"I have it now," I said. "It needs to be returned. It's my reputation on the line."

"Yes, because you've been nothing but professional up to now."

I swallowed down. I wasn't proud of him being threatened, but he was alive.

"Heads up," came the Wire's voice through my earpiece. "There's a security team congregating by Ray's table."

I checked my watch. "Bad news," I said to everybody listening, both local and remote. "Ray's getting antsy about his investment. I think he's angry with us."

"Speak for yourself," chuckled Cisco. "I wasn't the one who made a deal with the local devil."

Everybody turned to him and stared.

He went sober with a reluctant sigh. "Oh, all right. Let's go dance."

Dance Party

We exited into the dim hallway. The Heavy and the Lead brightened when they saw me, Bernard, and the client. Their gazes lingered on Cisco.

"He's a friend," I said. "It's a long story."

The animist seemed more interested in the open club door letting in smoke, blinking lights, and electronic beats that echoed down the walls. "What kind of music is this anyway? It sounds like ghost cats are dying."

The Lead pressed her lips together. "If they're ghosts then they can't die."

Cisco scoffed. "Trust me, ghosts can die."

I smiled at the necromancer. "The music is half the charm of a place like this."

"And what type of place is that?"

I blinked at him. As overbearing as he was, I had to remind myself that Cisco knew little about my world. "Apparently it's a playground for hellions, real or fake. It's best not to stare too closely, or you'll never scrub the nightmares from your mind."

He took the statement in stride and pragmatically considered my team. "Okay, why don't you all let me know what kind of spellcraft you're running."

The Heavy scrunched his brows and the Lead's tongue got stuck in her throat.

"They don't use magic."

"They're not animists?" His eyes were wide with disbelief. "Don't tell me you're planning on fighting through a crowd of hellions with fists and stun guns."

The Lead shrugged. "We usually get by."

"Yeah," agreed the Heavy, "though we don't usually find ourselves in places spinning ghost cat music."

Cisco grinned at him. The silvan was less amused.

"You all ready to get a move on?" reminded the Wire. "They're advancing on your position."

I cursed. "We've got incoming."

"Then let's get out of here," urged the client. "Might I remind you that my contract guarantees safe passage out of here?"

"He's right," said Cisco. "We should leave."

The Wire tapped at his keyboard. "I can get you an exit. There's a back door through the kitchen."

The Heavy turned to me. "The kitchen's closed this time of night. That back door sounds good."

"No," I said. "Ray gave us fifteen minutes to get the package back to him. If we don't deliver, we owe him."

"That's his plan," deduced Cisco.

"Right. And the last thing I'm gonna do is give him what

he wants."

Cisco wryly studied me. "So this is what you do, huh? Covert ops?"

"It's a living."

"Only as long as you stay alive."

"How about this?" suggested the Heavy. "The Lead takes the client out the back way. The rest of us charge Ray's table."

I checked my watch again. Four minutes left on the original fifteen-minute limit.

"I like the idea, big guy," said Cisco, "but you're no good in there with us." The Heavy's face flashed with anger.

"What he means," I cut in, "is we shouldn't leave the Lead and the client defenseless. You need to protect them."

"What about you?" he asked.

"I've got Bernard."

The gargoyle nodded affirmatively.

Cisco flashed his palms to the air. "What am I, chopped liver?"

"Time's running out," prodded the Wire. "Whatever you're gonna do, do it now."

"You heard him," I told the team. "Finish the job. Meet at the rendezvous."

The Heavy frowned but didn't object. He guided the silvan toward the kitchen. I watched my team walk away with a sigh. Things had gone sideways on us, but somehow a successful conclusion was within reach. Cisco, Bernard, and I marched the opposite way toward the door leading into the club. It was hanging open on its hinges after Bernard's rough treatment.

"These hellions," started Cisco, pacing to the door. "They're not gonna try to bargain for my soul or anything like that, right?"

"No, but they might try to eat your liver."

He wavered for a second, but a mask of confidence took over. "We'll see about that."

"You ready for this, Bernard?"

"It's literally why I was created," he answered.

"Fair enough."

Cisco led through the door followed by the gargoyle and me.

Distorted Latin vocals backed a synthwave soundscape. The dance floor swayed in harmony. Cisco pointed out a few of the white hellions with horns on the perimeter.

"Let's use the dance floor as cover," I said.

Instead of skirting around either side, we pushed right into the middle of the mass. It took only a few seconds for the blob to swallow us completely. Meanwhile, the Wire directed the rest of the team through the kitchen. It wasn't hard to tune out with the low beat vibrating the floor.

Bernard was as solid as they came, but he was only the height of a large dog. He helped clear the way but couldn't shield me completely. A serpentine tongue rolled up my arm and shoulder. I flinched away and kept moving. Cisco was a few steps away, assertively pushing through as long red nails caressed his upper arms.

Well, at least we were both being objectified.

Presumptuous as the crowd was, it provided excellent

cover. We made it across the dance floor and past a few pursuers before they ever saw us. We emerged on the other side.

A red-skinned woman with circlets stretching her ten-inch neck pointed at us. "That's them!"

A large rhinoceros of a man spun around. His skin was gray and heavily plated, and though he didn't sport a horn, his nose could've been mistaken for one.

"So much for the B team," I called out.

Bernard slammed into the oversize enforcer before he could focus on us. Despite being a quarter his size, the gargoyle toppled him. Clubgoers parted as the two skidded across the floor.

Two whitehorns charged us. Cisco threw his hands up and a ball of shadow blasted them off their feet.

The woman swung her heel into my wrist, knocking the stun gun away. We watched it slide onto the dance floor and disappear beneath a mass of legs. She turned to me, pinkie on pouting lips, with a hint of canine fangs showing. "I'm sorry. Was that for me, darling?"

"Nope."

I went into my jacket, pulled out an ASP, and flicked my wrist. The black baton extended into two feet of solid metal.

"This one's for you."

I cracked her across the cheek, spinning her head around. She crumbled as Bernard was thrown into a wall separating the dance floor from the lounge area. The gargoyle's mass broke through the divider to the other side.

Cisco's shadows clutched the rhino demon around the

neck. The enforcer groaned and ripped the tethers of magic away.

"Hey, no fair," griped the shadow charmer.

The demon clamped a large mitt onto Cisco's head and lifted him from the floor. Muzzle flashes erupted as Cisco blind fired into his enemy's chest. Against the club's raucous kick drums, the pistol shots sounded like background snares, and they had less effect against the hellion's armor than on the music.

Bernard pulled through the hole in the wall and shook his body like a dog, shedding crumbling drywall. "I suppose I'd better go save the lug."

The megademon growled at his trouble crushing Cisco's skull. Bernard landed on his back and wedged stone claws into the base of his neck, digging into a crevice. He ripped an armored plate away, exposing a section of tender, sticky flesh.

"Okay, that's gross," said Bernard.

The demon released Cisco and spun around, brushing the gargoyle off his back. I moved toward the stepped entry into the lounge, scanning for threats.

The rhino demon pounded a fist into Bernard, who skidded several feet back, scratching deep grooves across the floor. The gargoyle kept his distance, looking for an opening. Cisco's pistol went off again. He emptied the mag and the demon recoiled and stumbled. His armor may have been bulletproof, but his soft flesh wasn't.

Cisco met my eyes. "Heads up!" he warned.

Three whitehorns congregated at the steps to the lounge

and approached, blocking access to Ray. Bernard and Cisco hurried over and prepared to fight.

"I've got a better idea," I said.

I led them to the hole in the wall Bernard had created and slipped through to the next room. With the rhino demon back on his feet, they quickly squeezed through. The whitehorns cursed and backtracked toward the steps. They wouldn't be able to reach us before we got to Ray.

"You see?" I gloated. "Brains beat brawn."

The entire wall buckled as the rhino demon rammed through it. He wasn't small enough to fit through Bernard's hole, but he was built enough to make his own. The rhino took a support beam with him and the entire wall collapsed.

"Tell that to the big guy," mugged Cisco.

Suddenly our escape wasn't looking nearly as sure.

VIP

Bernard pounced and the demon knocked him away. I slammed the ASP into his arm but the impact shook me more than him. Cisco shoved me backward. The demon swiped in retaliation, hitting him instead of me. The shadow charmer flew across the room, hit a table, and landed on his back. Man knew how to take a beating.

I stepped aside as Bernard rushed in again. He traded blows with the rhino as the whitehorns rushed into the room, flanking us.

I sneered across the lounge at Ray and his four women watching in rapt attention. All the bar's patrons were attentive to the show. Unsurprisingly, none moved to intervene.

"I think we need some help," I told Bernard.

He was hanging onto the megademon's arms as it pounded the floor. "I know what you're thinking, and it's too dangerous."

"The Dark One will make easy work of him."

Boom, boom, boom he went into the floor. "But at what cost?" *Boom, boom, boom.* "You always lose control."

I had to give it to the gargoyle. He was undersized, but he was indestructible.

Cisco shakily stood and reloaded his pistol. As he trudged over, he fired at the flanking whitehorns. The gunfire caused the entire room to cower behind tables, including the whitehorns. One was too slow and fell on his side, grimacing in pain.

When the gun ran empty, Cisco set it on a table and turned to the rhino demon. Bernard spun away, forcing it to split his attention between them.

The Wire's voice came over the radio. "One minute, Handler. Get the package to Ray."

"Do it," growled Bernard.

I backed away, hesitant to leave them behind but knowing it was the smart play. The second I returned the package to its owner, the game was over. Ray would have no more cause to attack us. He likely viewed the whole affair as sport anyway.

I made for the VIP table, pulling the Sigillum Dei pendant from under my shirt and letting it hang in plain sight. I wasn't sure how much power the amulet had against these hellions, but it was worth a shot. As the seconds ticked on, synth music crescendoed against a women's melodic voice.

Just because Bernard and Cisco tag-teamed the big demon didn't mean I was in the clear. Two whitehorns came for me fast. One reached out, nearly on top of me. I kicked a vacant chair into his legs and stepped aside. He crashed to the ground beside me. Ray flinched as the ASP came down and split the whitehorn's nose open.

I spun as the second bore down. The downed whitehorn grabbed my boot and shoved it aside. I tumbled onto him, landing my elbow on his sternum. It knocked the wind from him, but he held me tight. Up close, his gasping mouth released rancid breath through several sets of teeth.

I recoiled. I was wrapped up by one demon while another was converging, but there was no slipping out. I was trapped. Leaning close, I thrust the Sigillum Dei onto his chest and cursed him.

A bright gout of flame erupted beneath my palm. I rolled away as the fire consumed the whitehorn from head to toe as if he were soaked in gasoline. Tables knocked to the floor as patrons fled the area. Even the other whitehorn backed away, fear in his eyes.

At the far wall, both Cisco and Bernard had been knocked away. The rhino demon saw me recover and move for Ray. He growled, lowered his head, and barreled toward me, knocking away any tables or patrons in his path.

I leapt over a low wall and sprinted to the VIP table. Ray was absolutely glowing with excitement. Obstacles exploded behind me but I couldn't bear to look. I was almost at the table when fat fingers snagged my hair. The megademon stopped me short and twisted me around.

He was big. He was ugly. His large nose appeared broken, but his armored hide had protected him from the brunt of the beating. He didn't even look bothered by the bullets surely embedded in his back.

But man was he angry.

His free hand came at me like I was a bug that needed squashing. Bernard swooped in and dragged his arm to the floor. The demon grunted in annoyance. He looked from the gargoyle, to me, and then to Ray.

But the last thing he saw was the tip of a glowing purple sword emerge from his chest cavity. The demon released my hair and gaped drop-jawed as blood poured from his body. When he collapsed forward to the ground, Cisco stood behind, a blade of dark energy flowing from his hand. He dispelled the spellcraft and the battle was over.

I blinked stupidly, even more impressed than the demon had been.

"Handler," pressed Bernard, using my code name in front of the others.

I spun around and slapped the summoning marker to the table right in front of the club owner.

"Seconds to spare, I believe."

Ray's lips twitched together. "Assuredly."

"The contract's over. Call off your minions."

He scooped up his treasure and raised both eyebrows. "My dear, you don't think these are mine, do you? Whyever would I hurt you?"

I snorted as Bernard and Cisco joined me at the table. The animist wiped blood from his mouth. "Who says we're hurt?"

Ray chuckled. "A turn of phrase. Despite the unfortunate incident, you handled yourself impressively."

"Didn't know she had an animist with her, did you?" taunted Cisco.

"I was talking about the pendant," he said, locking eyes with me. "How did you do that?"

I slipped the Sigillum Dei back under my shirt. "Trade secret."

"But then, I deal in secrets, don't I? And you're overlooking something."

I kept my business face on. "What's that?"

"If it had been me responsible for accosting you, why would I ever let you go after killing my brute?"

One of the three women sitting in the booth on his right jabbed a sawed-off shotgun into his ribs. "Self preservation," she suggested.

Ray's eyes flashed, and I realized I'd seen the woman before. Latina, with flawless tanned skin, wavy brown hair, and a full figure if I ever saw one. It was a year ago, and only for a moment, but she was unmistakable. I glared in Cisco's general direction.

"Wonderful," clapped Ray, not annoyed in the slightest. "Done in by my penchant for new faces. But do you presume that paltry weapon would kill me?"

Cisco grinned. "Do you presume it's loaded with standard shells?"

He squirmed a bit. "Perhaps not, but the question still stands."

The woman with the shotgun hiked a shoulder. "Does it really matter? Even if it didn't kill you, it would be pretty embarrassing. This is your joint, right?"

The club owner studied her with a hungry smile that showed his teeth. "Mmm, I was wondering about you, you know. You smell"—he sniffed—"intoxicatingly familiar."

The comment unnerved her, but she had a lot where that came from. Being on the giving end of a standoff can do that.

"It was a profitable job," I told Ray. "You got paid for fifteen minutes of time, got your marker back, and watched a nice show to boot. Let's all walk out of here in one piece."

Cisco chortled and set his alligator boot on the overturned rhino demon. "Well, most of us, anyway."

The brute rasped weakly and twisted his head to the wizard. Cisco hopped away in startled shock, apparently learning a valuable lesson about how hard hellions are to kill. Ray grinned, and I matched it.

"What do you say?" I prodded. "Friends?"

He took a deep breath and fluttered his eyelids. "As you wish. I give you my leave. You may exit untouched."

Cisco snorted as if he didn't need permission. "Come on, Milena. Time to go."

The beauty chuckled. "This place is dead anyway."

She slid from the booth and handed Cisco's gun back with a kiss. I didn't catch what he did with it but it disappeared from sight, which must've been a handy trick for the police.

We didn't dally on the way to the door.

Riding in the Rain

I unsummoned Bernard before leaving the basement. We strolled through the guts of a shuttered industrial building in silence until we made it outside. It was the early a.m. but still dark, though you wouldn't have guessed it from the busy bar inside. Not only did the Puzzle Box break the laws of the universe, they snubbed the local liquor regulations too. A light rain sprinkled down, glossing over the street.

"Looks like you brought the weather with you from Miami," I grumbled.

I headed to the mostly empty parking lot across the street and Cisco and Milena stayed in step with me. They were probably parked in the same place. My eye landed on the brown van in the corner of the lot.

I put the mic to my mouth. "Wire, the show's over. It was aces."

"That's our girl. The Heavy and the Lead are loaded up."

"And the silvan?"

"Went on his way."

Cisco watched with a smirk as we communicated. "Good. Get out of here. Go to the rendezvous without me."

"Uh, the Custodian's not gonna like that."

"He'll like it even less if I bring a tail to the meet. Just go. The job was a success. You got the information over the mic. I'll see you when I can."

The Wire sighed. "I hope you know what you're doing, Handler."

"I almost never do, Wire." I smiled as I shut the mic off and pulled the earpiece. I wrapped the wire around the tiny transmitter box and shoved it into the pocket of my jeans. The van pulled away as we trudged into the lot.

"You're like a secret agent," teased Cisco. "What's with this Wire, Handler stuff?"

For a second I thought he'd somehow overheard the communication, but I realized Bernard had used my code name before. "None of us know each other's names," I explained.

"No honor among thieves, huh?"

I didn't say anything. I was good at what I did, even if it wasn't the most honorable profession. Cisco was a bleeding heart. His optimistic ideals made me feel a bit of shame. Then again, he was far from squeaky clean himself.

In this world, knowing the things we know, you do what it takes to get by.

"This is me," announced Cisco, strutting up to a white Jeep Wrangler with a black hard top.

I stopped and waited as the Wire turned down a distant

corner. "Okay, we're alone. We can talk freely."

"What, here? No offense but I thought we'd create a little distance between ourselves and the club full of demons."

"Plus the rain might get heavier," said Milena.

I chuckled. "This drizzle is the most we'll get for a month. Where would you have us go?"

Cisco shrugged. "Your place?"

"Nice try."

"You owe us. We saved that job for you. Besides, we'll find where you're holed up eventually."

I grumbled. "Fine. Follow me."

I moved to the Ducati a few spaces away and pulled on my helmet.

"Hey, wait a minute," he called. "What happened to the Beamer?"

"That was a company car. This one's mine."

"You're not gonna try to slip us, are you?"

I shrugged and straddled the bike.

"I'll ride with you," suggested Milena.

She was wearing a small party dress and high heels. The dress already strained at her curves. There was absolutely no room for hidden weapons.

"Hold on tight," I said.

She jumped behind me and I pulled out. Cisco hurried to get into his Jeep and keep up. Once on the street, I sped up for a short burst just to make him sweat, but then I played nice.

I still wasn't sure how I felt about them being here. I *had* been avoiding Cisco's calls. He was guaranteed trouble, and I should've been a bundle of nerves. At the same time, the guy wore his heart on his sleeve. I didn't trust him, but he wasn't running a scam on me. I was too savvy for that. I swallowed uncomfortably. What did that say about me?

But then, maybe I was avoiding Cisco for more practical reasons. I'd recently learned the truth about my boss. Bedrock was just a front man. The rest of the team reported to him and thought the Custodian was just another operator. Really? The Custodian was the man behind the man. The actual one in charge, pulling all our strings under the guise of our harmless coordinator.

It was a twisted charade, made even worse because I was forced to participate in it. The truth was, putting Cisco anywhere near my precarious mess was dangerous to him and his girlfriend.

The bike stopped at a red light and Milena opted for small talk.

"So, you're an animist?"

I frowned. It was weird to talk about it with other people, especially strangers. Then again, if she was with Cisco, she knew more than enough.

"I don't really think of myself like that," I said, "but I guess so. I don't shoot magic from my fingers or anything so flashy. I just have a knack for contacting hellions."

"That fire looked pretty flashy to me."

I snickered. That had been the work of the Sigillum Dei. The gold pentacle was meant for protection, but I'd used it offensively before. According to the demon on the receiving end, the power stemmed from me being a daughter of Solomon. So maybe I was flashier than I thought.

"I wish I knew magic. It must be cool," she mused, "being part of a team, having minions at your beck and call, and kicking ass."

I was quiet a moment. I resented the comment for some reason. Maybe it was because she was a tourist in my world. Maybe it was because she was too pretty. Geez, I hoped it wasn't so easy to get under my skin.

But maybe, I thought, it was because my life was anything but desirable. This was about survival. About scratching and clawing out a living. It was about saving my father and sticking it to those who've harmed us.

The traffic light flicked green and I was miles away from a solution.

"Not everything's as simple as it looks," was all I said.

I gunned the throttle of the Ducati Monster 821 so it was too loud to talk. Milena keyed in on my discomfort and we rode the rest of the way in silence.

As the gate of my underground parking garage opened, the Jeep pulled alongside me and Cisco buzzed down the window.

"Penthouse three," I told him. I rolled inside while he parked on the street.

On the sixth floor, I unlocked and propped the door open. We were back in my industrial loft. The sun was beginning to shine through pebbles of water on the wall of windows. Usually I'd be snuggled up in bed by this time. The thought made me yawn.

"This is a cool pad," offered Milena. "Very hip. Not like my place. New construction is so boring."

"Really? I would've thought with Cisco's money he would've sprung for something... flashier."

She smiled. "Oh, he did. Lives in a penthouse too, actually. But I have my own place."

"Oh." I nodded. I didn't know why I'd assumed they lived together. "So you guys aren't that serious?"

She sighed. "That's a complicated question."

Her face intimated more and I was immediately uncomfortable. I chided myself for the prying small talk. Why had I asked? That wasn't like me. Though Milena seemed a sociable person; she had a way of making you let your guard down. Maybe I'd find myself like Ray had, with a shotgun to my stomach.

Cisco walked in and I cleared my throat.

"So your team's out of the picture?" he asked. "Just like that?" He'd left the door open.

"Not just like that. I can stall them for maybe an hour, but I can't put them off forever. We need to debrief... Look at the next steps."

I summoned Bernard. He appeared beside the door and kindly shut it. Cisco jumped and spun around. "Damn. That's freaky."

"What's the matter?" asked the gargoyle. "Afraid of a little scuffle?"

"Just keep that tail where I can see it, mutt." He stepped away from my familiar and I grinned. It was fun to watch him squirm a bit.

"Why don't we get down to business and discuss what you're doing here?"

"Is the... gargoyle gonna stick around for this?"

"Why not?"

"Maybe 'cause he's a murderous hellion?"

Milena chuckled. "I think he's cute."

Cisco traded glances between the two of us. "So what, you just keep this thing around as a pet?"

"I trust Bernard way more than I trust you, bub."

"That hurts, Shyla." He put his back to the sofa, safely away from the gargoyle, and hooked his hands on his hips, not quite comfortable enough to sit. "So you were saying? What next steps are your team taking?"

I shook my head. "Uh-uh. I asked you first. You're in my town, in my loft. You've been calling me. It's about time you told me why."

He finally sat on the couch, spreading his elbows across the back to show how casual he was. "Can't a guy lie low outside Miami a bit?"

"Probably smart, considering the Shadow Man news reports I've seen. But you said you were working something, following that silvan for a reason."

"Might as well tell her, Cisco," interjected Milena as she strolled over to the other side of the sectional and lay down. "It's why we're here."

I couldn't believe she was still in her heels and she still looked amazing. Even on her back, her breasts were larger than mine. She was *so* Cisco's type.

I crossed my arms. "Well?"

"Okay, screw it," he said, pulling his arms onto his knees and leaning forward. "This is hard for me to say, so let's not make a big deal about it, okay?"

My eyes narrowed. "What's hard to say?"

He glanced at Milena, but she was smiling while resting her eyes, unwilling to give him the slightest bit of support. "You guys are gonna make me actually say it."

I audibly huffed. "Say what, Cisco?"

He cleared his throat. "Fine. When it comes down to it, I guess... I have to say... I could use your help."

Get by With a Little Help From My Friends

I burst out laughing. "That's it? That's what was so hard for you to say?" Milena giggled right along with me.

It was such a stereotype, but that was Cisco. The macho Cuban guy, big muscles and big heart, but kind of a loner at times. An "I'll take care of it" do-it-yourselfer. No problem was too big for his force of will to surmount, nobody put one past him, and it really—*really*—hurt to ask for help.

It was about the funniest thing I'd ever seen.

"Thanks for not making this hard," he grumped.

I straightened my face and waved it off. "It's just that... You realize I'm a contractor, right? It's literally my job to do jobs for people. I'm a summoner for hire."

He canted his head to concede the obvious point. I felt mercy for him and moved on.

"Just tell me what's going on. I read about that serial killer business in your city."

"That's where it started, actually. I trapped the guy's soul after he died. Just for a minute. I interrogated him, and he thought he was sent by angels."

I grimaced at the word.

"There's a group of black witches I've been trying to track down, and they're anything but angels." His face went dark. "I found one of them in the Nether. They're hellions from Stygia."

I traded a look of concern with Bernard. But it was just a thought. I raised my chin, curiosity piqued. "And you know this how?"

"That's what she said."

"She said Stygia?"

"Definitely."

"Hmm, hellions are rarely so straightforward."

"Yeah," he said, and his brash smile returned. "She was a little cocky. They've got a superiority complex. She thought I was a dead man."

Curious choice of words for a necromancer. And I could sympathize. Going toe to toe with a hellion was scary business. "How'd you manage to escape?" I asked.

"Oh God," said Milena. "You set him up."

"Escape?" gloated Cisco. "She was the one who escaped from me."

Milena scoffed but Cisco ignored it. Something about his expression told me he wasn't just telling stories. I started to wonder if Cisco could help me too.

"They're called stiges," he said. "They're creepy witches with black owl consorts. Heard of 'em?"

I nudged one of the lounge chairs along the polished concrete and sat across from them. "Unfortunately, no. Hell is a twisted realm, spanning multiple rings, numerous cities and strongholds, and more beings than the Animal Kingdom. But that doesn't mean I can't find out."

His obvious disappointment waned a little. "How?"

I spread my hands to the air. "I have contacts. It just takes a little digging, but if these stiges are powerful, someone will have heard of them."

"And you can find out what they're up to? Why they're interested in the Earthly Steppe?"

He was talking about the Material Plane now. "I thought you met them in the Nether?"

"I did, but they sent the serial killer to expose animists. That's what the TV coverage is about. The stiges have hooks in the vampire underworld and the silvan kingdom too."

I considered his statements with a healthy dose of skepticism. Hellions weren't allowed to play in our world. The Elemental Planes, maybe, but here?

Then again, I had just spent the night in the Puzzle Box. A week ago I would've sworn that place was impossible.

But Cisco wasn't talking about a controlled environment. He was talking about hellions loose in the city. There had to be more to that story. My first instinct was to go after their summoner.

"I can do the job," I said. "I won't even charge you if I don't find anything."

"Wait, wait, wait," tempered Cisco. "Hold on a minute. What do you mean 'charge'?"

My reply was that of a cool professional. "You're hiring

me for a job. That involves expenses."

"I'll cover anything out of pocket, but you've taken enough of my money."

"I worked for that."

"You stole it. Bags of money. From me."

"We're square on that."

"We're square when I say we're square. You still have plenty of my cash squirreled away somewhere, so I say you still owe me."

Bernard growled aggressively. The last thing I wanted was for this to turn into a fight, especially when things were going so well. That didn't mean I could afford to be impractical. Cisco was wrong about me still having his money. I didn't even have enough to cover my payment to the Custodian this month. A cool quarter million, or I was in the doghouse. I'd been hoping Mr. Moneybags here could spot me a little more.

"I don't live my life paying off debts," I said. It was a big old lie, plain and simple. My entire life was payback for a mistake my father had made. Now I belonged to the Custodian and there wasn't an end in sight.

Which didn't mean I didn't feel for Cisco's plight. I had rules, and one of them was not to steal from anyone who didn't have it coming. I had initially thought Cisco was some big bad outlaw. Maybe he fit the bill, but he wasn't about personal gain. Taking out a serial killer? Sniffing after intrusive hellions? He didn't need to do those things.

Cisco's face softened. "There's... there's something else. It's Milena."

Until now, she'd been comfortably lounging on the sidelines of our conversation. Now she shuffled nervously.

"She was poisoned by the stiges," he continued. "By all accounts, she should be dead right now. It seems like we took care of most of the lingering effects, but..."

Concern crept over my face. "But what?"

"Well, we're not sure..."

Milena sat up. "If there's something wrong with me?" she finished.

Cisco winced. "Baby, you said it yourself. The Nether's calling to you. It's how we found the silvan messenger. Their glamours are nearly impossible to crack. He looked human to me. But Milena? She saw right through it somehow."

He shook his head, forlorn. "Sometimes she feels uncomfortable in the sunlight. We're from Miami. She loves the beach." He waited a breath. "We think—we were told—that she isn't human anymore."

My gaze fell on Milena. "I'm sorry," was all I could say.

She sucked her teeth and stood. "I can't talk about this now."

"You heard Ray," Cisco pleaded. "You have a connection with something dark. We need to find out what that is."

"I feel fine." Milena paced away from the couch, then lifted her eyes to the door. "I think I'm gonna go for a walk."

"It's dawn," he said.

"Don't wait up."

The suddenly agitated woman let herself out. I wondered

if there was more going on here than I thought. I turned to Cisco, surprised he wasn't following her.

"Let her blow off some steam," he said dejectedly. "She's a big girl. Besides, I wouldn't wanna be next to her when she finds out this town doesn't have Cuban coffee."

I wasn't sure how to respond to his cool comments. The man took the entire world in stride. It was the same reason I kept myself busy with work. As long as I focused on the current job, eyes forward, I didn't need to fret over the big picture.

Things were clearly different when someone was hurt or in danger. That demanded attention, and I felt myself sympathizing with Cisco even more.

"Aw, hell," I groaned.

"Don't do it, Shyla," pressed Bernard.

"How can I not?"

The gargoyle approached and lowered his voice. "How can you afford to?"

"So what? We'll cut it close this month. It isn't the end of the world."

Cisco arched an eyebrow. "You two mind telling me what you're going on about?"

"I'll do the job," I told him. "I'm doing this because she needs help, because my heart isn't completely withered to dust yet."

Cisco cautiously smiled.

"I'm also doing this to erase my debt. I go down this path with you, give it my best shot, and no matter the outcome, we're even. Got it? Because if you can't square with that then—"

"It's a deal," he said. "Trust me, I know there are no guarantees in life. All I ask is that you try."

I stopped myself from saying more. For some reason his sappy sentiment caught me off guard. He was like an episode of *Supernatural* or something. Endearing despite itself.

"So any ideas?" he asked.

"On what?"

"The stiges."

I sighed. "Well, I know hellions can't come into Creation uninvited."

"Creation?"

I groggily rubbed my eyes. "Yeah, you know, what you call the steppes. Your stiges will be working with a summoner of some sort."

"Could it be a silvan? I found out the hard way their high king was in league with them, if only to protect his people."

I wasn't sure. I'd never heard of a netherling summoner.

"Which reminds me..." he wondered aloud. "I shouldn't be the first one asking about this. One of the silvan circles, the Circle of Bone, tried contacting you about it."

"Me?"

"It's what you do, right?"

I twisted my lips. I didn't have any contacts in that kingdom, but there was one person who did. The same one who'd picked up the latest job at the Puzzle Box.

"It must've gone through my boss, the Custodian," I said. "He's hooked into that world."

"Then we need to wonder why he never mentioned it to you." Cisco mulled it over and nodded as he came to his decision. "I'm not sure you can trust this guy."

I laughed sharply at the understatement of the year. "Oh, I *definitely* can't trust him. You don't know the half of it."

The problem was, I couldn't tell him the half of it. The details of my boss and my servitude were a trade secret of sorts. I wasn't free to go blabbing about it to anyone. The knowledge would put me and those who knew in danger.

"Look, it's complicated," I non-explained. "It shouldn't affect our investigation. And we have a few avenues of inquiry. I'm not sure if it means anything, but I recently found out the hard way that Stygia changed leadership. I was told our world was starting to feel the fallout from that."

His eyes lit up. "That's something."

"Might be," I said to temper his expectations. "It might be nothing. Like I said, Hell's complicated."

A text message came in. It was the Wire, reporting that everything had gone well. No need for me to see them tonight. The sudden freedom hit me like a heavy wave, and I realized how tired I was.

"Let's pick this up later," I suggested. "Maybe we can still salvage some shut-eye."

"Sounds good to me. Listen, in case I need to go down and check on Milena, can I get a spare key?"

My immediate refusal stuck in my throat as I realized he wanted to sleep over. "I thought you've been in town for weeks. Don't you already have a hotel or something?"

He grimaced sheepishly. "I *did*. The thing about that is I kinda set off the fire alarm and caused several thousand dollars worth of smoke damage."

I glared at him.

"Hey, I wasn't bluffing Ray before. I really did put special cartridges in that shotgun." He shrugged. "I was prepping the rounds a little quick and dirty with local supplies and one thing led to another..."

I stopped him with my hand. "Okay, fine. Take the couch. You don't need a key. Bernard's better than any lock." I pulled my jacket off and headed toward the bed. "Just don't try to come in the bedroom. And no voodoo."

I sat on the bed, Cisco still visible past the bookshelf dividing the open floor plan, and pulled off my boots. The gargoyle took up position between us, standing guard at the entrance to my private space like an eternal sentinel. He wouldn't budge until I did.

Staging

I woke up to arguing voices with harsh sunlight streaming through the windows.

"But you wanted to come," insisted Cisco.

"Maybe I changed my mind," returned Milena.

"Maybe you're scared."

"Of course I'm scared! Aren't you?"

I begrudgingly lifted my head and peeped around. "Morning, Bernard."

His tail flicked. "It's nearly noon." His British accent was especially haughty at the moment, probably due to the sound pollution. Still wearing last night's gear, I pushed out of bed, grabbed some new clothes, and disappeared into the bathroom.

I came out refreshed, wearing a Grateful Dead shirt that I hoped would chill the mood, and found that the argument had ended. Look at that, the Dead were already doing their work. I emerged into the living room, finding Cisco at the kitchen counter pouring a fresh pot of coffee.

"Make yourself at home," I said, although it was hard to be mad as the scent wafted my way. He grabbed an extra mug and poured me one.

Cisco wore jeans and a white tank top, as he always did. "Sorry for waking you up. Milena... This thing isn't easy to deal with. She has her on and off days."

I couldn't remember most of what they'd said, but it wasn't my business anyway. I scooted across the floor in socks and accepted my black ambrosia. I was willing to forgive a lot for that little token of peace. "Where is she?"

"She wanted to try that breakfast place downstairs."

"It's good."

"And the bar."

I snickered. "That's good too." And then a thought. "Did she sleep?"

"That's on and off too."

Bernard strutted near us with an idle stretch.

"You know," said Cisco, "that pet of yours didn't move a muscle. He was a literal statue."

"Nice of you to notice," remarked the gargoyle.

A dainty knock rapped my front door. Cisco's face washed with relief as he hurried to answer it. Strange since the door was still unlocked. I reached for my phone but I'd left it on the nightstand.

"Wait," I called. I went and opened the door myself.

It was the Lead in a sun dress. She had a fresh coat of makeup on and her curled blonde hair was well-styled, without even a hint of having been in a ratty smoke-filled basement all night. Her smile announced to the whole world that she was a morning person, and I hated her.

I was also stunned that she knew where I lived.

"What are you doing here?" I asked snidely.

"The Custodian said you volunteered your place as our staging ground." She brushed inside and hardly gave Bernard a nod. Her eyes fluttered at my muscled guest, though. "And here's the mystery man of the hour." She held her hand out. "We never formally met."

"Cisco. You?"

"I'm the Lead, silly."

He arched an unamused eyebrow. I stepped outside the doorway and checked up and down the hall. Nobody else incoming. I returned inside. "The Custodian said what?"

"I was surprised too," she admitted. "Even more now that I see the place. Between the beautiful loft and this hunk of a man, I'm a little jealous. I didn't know you had it in you, Handler."

I didn't have time for the Lead's banter. I was still grumbling at the Custodian's suggestion to open my loft to the team. He was doing it to get on my nerves, no doubt. To punish me for not showing last night or just to keep me in check. Bedrock was the technical owner of the penthouse, so my anonymity wasn't compromised, but it still felt like a violation.

The elevator dinged through the open door and I peeked my head out again. Sure enough, there was the Wire. He was a stocky Chinese man in his forties with hoop earrings and one of those taxi driver hats. His laid-back Gen X appearance revealed no clues to his technical expertise or vocation.

"Welcome to the party," I said as he arrived.

He gave me a quick bro hug. "That was hairy last night, huh?"

I left the door open and walked him in. "The Heavy coming by too?"

"Nah, he's sitting this one out with twenty stitches and a concussion."

I grimaced. "I didn't realize."

"He's fine. It's a free vacation. Besides, word is this next phase will require more tact than his talents allow." The Wire's step stuttered when he realized Cisco was in the room, but the surprise wore off quickly. "I guess I have to thank you for last night." He offered his hand and shook Cisco's.

"All in a day's work," said the shadow charmer.

The Wire smiled. "Sure. Hey, I hope you don't mind me asking what you're doing here though?"

"Good question," came the Custodian's voice.

I spun to the door. I hadn't heard the elevator ding. He eyed me as he pointedly shut the door, indicating the gathering of the team was complete. The Custodian, the Handler, the Wire, the Lead... and Cisco.

The Custodian was a precise man. He had light gray eyes, a long face, and a strong jaw with a cleft chin. His wire glasses actually helped soften his demeanor, but overall he couldn't shake the appearance of being uptight. He was the only one in the room wearing a button-up, and the part and wave in his gelled hair were more meticulously done than the Lead's.

"Visiting hours are over," he said coldly.

Cisco almost snorted like a bull, watching the Custodian with hard eyes.

I inserted myself between them. "I think he should stay."

"Impossible," said the Custodian. "Bedrock wouldn't be happy."

By Bedrock, of course, he meant himself, but he still had to put on a show for the rest of the team. That act worked to my advantage, however, because I could publicly push him back. The Wire and the Lead thought the Custodian was just another team member, an equal among equals.

The truth was, he was more dangerous than Cisco. Even with all my talents and familiars, the Custodian was basically untouchable.

It didn't mean he held all the cards.

"Well," I announced loudly, "after graciously volunteering my loft as the crew's staging area, I had a little chat with Bedrock."

His eyes narrowed. The first part of my statement had been his lie, but the second was my own. We were bluffing each other back and forth, because only the two of us knew the truth about the team.

"Meet our newest operator, the Shadow."

Cisco was almost as upset as the Custodian, but the animist's ire was mostly due to the lame code name. I thought it was appropriate considering his recent news coverage. And while I knew some of the team had caught his real name already, I had to do what I could to protect his identity from the Custodian...

Who was angrily working his jaw.

"Is this a joke?"

"Not at all. He was Bedrock's idea, actually. I'm just following orders."

I gave him a sardonic smile. Bedrock wasn't allowed to make unilateral decisions like that. It was an open lie, which was a small risk because he could've called me on it. If he really wanted to screw me in front of the team, he could, but he had to consider the cost of doing so.

It was the Custodian who had started this game. And we both knew, as long as I didn't push too hard, he wouldn't break up the band. In this case, I didn't think it was worth my head.

"A word please," he said.

Ignoring the inquisitive stares of the team, he pulled me over to the kitchen. The open floor plan didn't give adequate privacy for a bitch-out session, so we composed ourselves and spoke in hushed whispers.

"What does he know?" he asked.

"About what?"

"Us."

"Nothing. He knows me from an old job in Miami."

"Miami?" The Custodian nodded. "Does he perhaps have anything to do with the reason you refuse to ever work in Miami again?"

"Pfft. It's the humidity. It frizzes my hair."

"Why's he here, Shyla?"

I swallowed at his familiar use of my real name. I didn't

like it, and I refused to use his. "I found him at the Puzzle Box. He was already onto the silvan. Look, it's better for the team to think we put him there on purpose instead of it being a happy accident. It makes us look like we know what we're doing. Plus, he can help us."

The Wire and the Lead had respectfully kept their distance, but by this point Cisco was approaching. The Custodian clenched his jaw and hurried away. Cisco's shoulder brushed into his not incidentally, and they squared up with each other.

I tensed. Cisco might've been a harder-than-usual tough guy, but he had no idea who he was dealing with here.

"My bad," said the animist with a crude smile. "I must not have seen you. Is there a problem?" Then he leaned forward and added in a whisper. "I'm going to this convocation anyway, so you might as well have me on the official team."

Even Bernard watched the events closely. Cisco's brazen act meant he was oblivious to the Custodian's true identity, and the whole thing was likely to explode in his face.

Luckily, the same charade that cast the Custodian as our harmless middle manager prevented him from flexing his true muscle. In front of the team, Cisco was safe.

My boss cleared his throat. "Just a small misunderstanding on my part. I'm told you performed admirably last night."

It was obvious to me he nearly choked on the words, but it was convincing enough for the rest of the team.

"You have all met the Shadow by this point," announced

the Custodian to them, stealing my thunder. "I assure you, he's a capable worker. We'll be sure to put him to good use."

He eyed Cisco in warning with that statement, showing he intended to deliver on that promise.

"And the best news," he added, "is his addition won't affect your pay scales at all. The Shadow's in this one as a personal favor to Bedrock. He's not getting paid so there's no money out of your pockets."

The Wire grinned. "Then let me be the first to say welcome aboard, brother!"

I snorted as we all congregated around the large sectional. It was a nice counterpunch on his part. He was gonna make Cisco work, and it was gonna be for nothing. I'm sure I would deal with the consequences later as well, but it couldn't be helped.

"So what's the next phase?" inquired the Lead, eager to move on. "Do I get to wear a gown?"

"Of course you do," returned the Custodian. "And to answer the more important question: We're going to steal a scepter."

The Convocation

I sat in the chair I had pulled up to the couch the night before. The Lead and the Wire took places on the sectional. Since the Custodian was addressing the group, he stood before us. Not to be one-upped, Cisco took up position against one of the few interior walls in the loft, the frame of the master bathroom. He crossed his arms over his chest and planted a shoulder into the wall.

"Last night," began the Custodian, "we learned of a convocation."

"But you already knew that," shot Cisco, "because you already wanted to steal the scepter."

Great. Cisco couldn't go more than one sentence without interrupting. It was going to be interesting having him on the team.

The Custodian gave a firm nod. "Yes, actually, but we didn't know the time or place. We have that now. The Conway House is an upscale landmark owned by a trust in the philanthropic family's name. The actual Conway son is little involved in day-to-day operations. On the night in question, a charity banquet is scheduled on the property for a non-profit called Helping Home. They provide houses to the homeless."

The Wire mimicked the organization's tagline from an ad campaign. "A helping hand starts with a home."

"That's the one."

"Wait a minute," said the Lead. "A... silvan from one elemental plane contacts a demon in another... just so they can attend a charity for homeless people?"

Her eyes lingered on me but I didn't offer any insight yet. The Lead strolls through a place like the Puzzle Box and sees demons everywhere. Maybe she wasn't far off, but the things living in the elemental planes weren't hellions, per se.

The Custodian pressed his lips together a moment. "Organizations like these are often used for illicit purposes. Money laundering, extortion schemes, what have you."

The familiarity with which he spoke made me think he might be involved in several such organizations. The owner of my loft, Bedrock Manufacturing, for example. Ironically, they were my favorite kind of people to steal from.

"Knowing what we do about the supernatural world," he continued, "you can imagine how beneficial it would be for non-human actors to control very human enterprises."

The Lead scoffed. "So what happens to all the homeless people?!?"

The Custodian cocked his head. "You don't think, when you hand money over to a charity, that the people in need actually see more than cents on the dollar, do you?"

Cisco snorted. "He's right. Don't get me started on where your blood goes when you give to the American Red Cross."

A curious twinkle caught in the Custodian's eye, like maybe there was something to the muscled gym rat in a tank top.

As for Cisco's statement about the blood, everyone was too afraid to ask.

"Forget the scams," prodded the Wire. "What about the scepter? Where does it fit in?"

The Custodian nodded. "Some of the guests at the banquet will be of the supernatural variety. A coming together of parties on neutral ground, if you will. One of these parties will carry a golden scepter. I don't have many details, but I'm told it's a valuable family heirloom."

"That's all we know?" I asked.

"All that matters is that Bedrock wants the scepter."

"Okay," said the Wire, keeping up. "Who is it we're stealing from?"

"That's the last piece of the puzzle," revealed the Custodian, "made complicated for several reasons." He adjusted the glasses on his aquiline nose and sized me up. "Handler, everyone in attendance is well familiar with your affinity for hellions, but they're perhaps less aware of a summoner's link to the elemental planes. Why don't you give them a primer?"

I nodded, knowingly exactly what complication he was getting at. But first, the team needed the proper background.

"It's said that during the creation of the Earth," I started, "the elements were split apart. Fire and air were ripped from the ether to create the High Elemental Plane, a home for primal beings of elemental power."

Cisco chortled. "Trust me, you don't want any piece of those guys."

I glared at him pointedly before resuming. "As a consequence of the split, an equal and opposite plane formed below our world from the leftovers of water and earth. The Low Elemental Plane, almost by neglect, became the de facto home of races twisted from mankind. Neither world is Hell, and none of their residents are demons."

The Lead and the Wire listened with the casual interest of hearing another fairy tale. I knew Cisco was familiar with the Aether and the Nether, as many animists called the elemental planes, but he seemed genuinely curious as I recited the legendary origins.

"At the Puzzle Box," I continued, "it wasn't a demon I summoned, it was an elemental aspect. You can think of them as sentient servants. It wasn't the target of the message, just another middleman. And as I'm sure he was instructed, the silvan broke the circle and let the elemental loose."

"Is it dangerous?" asked the Lead.

"Probably, but that's not the worst part. It being loose means we have no means to track who it delivers its message to. And it's safe to say if it was for a vanilla human, the silvans could've just used the post office. The elemental is a messenger formed from the base Intrinsics, able to move without a trace if needed, and it's sending along an invite to one or more supernatural parties."

The Custodian spread his hands. "That's about the sum of it. Any questions so far?"

"I got one," piped up the Wire, leaning forward and scratching the faintest impression of facial hair on his chin. "I understand the company, the cover, and the players, at least as well as I'll be able to, but why the need for the charade? Why not have this meeting in the middle of Antarctica without pesky humans around? For that matter, why not just conduct business in the elemental planes?"

"They can't," I answered. "Netherlings can't travel to the High, and jinns can't get into the Low. Not only is the Material Plane a neutral territory that gives neither side an advantage, but it would literally be impossible for them to meet anywhere else."

"Or close enough to be impractical," agreed the Custodian. "Besides that, these entities have plenty of business with *us vanilla humans* as well. They don't want to be isolated." He flashed me a self-satisfied grin as he savored the irony of passing off as one of us. "So then, let's get into the how."

He pulled out his phone and initiated the usual encrypted link. The Wire and the Lead took out theirs, and Bernard was kind enough to retrieve mine from the nightstand and hand it to me before retiring back to the foot of the bed.

I'd recently learned the Custodian sometimes tracked us

with the phones he supplied. I tried dumping mine in the trash and picking up my own, but he objected to the change. Company business requires company assets. Now I just made sure to carry two phones around. One for him and the other for my private business, like when I texted Trap. And if I wanted to sneak around the city without the Custodian knowing about it, I left his phone at the loft.

I joined the group share as the Custodian pushed images to us. The first few appeared to be published location shots of the Conway House: the sprawling lawn dressed up for a wedding, the facade of the old-fashioned mansion, and the large iron gates decorated with life-size lions.

The Custodian narrated the slideshow. "The Conway House is closed to the public but hosts numerous private events every month. From the street it's a walled compound. Past the heavy gate is a winding road up the hill to the driveway. The property is famous for its large, private lawn, behind the building and surrounded by high walls and bushes. There'll likely be several rows of tables and a stage against the fountain backdrop.

"Helping Home is the organizer of the event. They'll be responsible for admissions and security, which is sure to be proactive. Employees will be mingling and presenting, but the vast majority of guests will be contributing members. Helping Home classifies their donors into various groups. This banquet is open to gold patrons only. But things are not as straightforward as that."

He swiped ahead to indoor shots of lavishly styled entertaining areas. The floors were Spanish tile lined with hall and area rugs. Antique artwork tastefully adorned the walls, which were more spartan than I would've imagined. There was almost a time-capsule quality to the decoration of eighty years ago.

"There's a secret tier of patrons known as platinums." His eyes met mine. "No official list of platinum patrons exists, and it's likely our mark is on this tier, hence why we can't simply acquire a list of suspects."

"Dumb question," said the Wire with a half-raised hand. "If this tier isn't listed anywhere, how do we know it exists? There are some famous billionaires, Conway included, who are very publicly on the gold level."

The Custodian smiled. "Which begs the question: What does it take to be acccpted into the top?"

I ignored the sinking feeling in my gut. "They're not human," I guessed.

"Or at least sufficiently able and aware of the others to be special."

The Wire and the Lead looked at each other, probably having flashbacks from the Puzzle Box. "More silvans?" asked the Lead.

"Can't be," said Cisco. "I was at their wedding. The marriage was announced far and wide among their kind. This convocation has to be aimed at new players."

The Custodian nodded in bemused agreement. "For this charity event, platinum patrons can gain exclusive access to the indoor lounge. Besides the public areas we have pictures of, there's a rumored basement level where the real magic happens. This level of the Conway House is an open secret, an urban legend from more decadent times, though it has never been substantiated in the modern era. At any rate, organizations renting the property aren't given access to it, and its existence is always stoutly denied."

He paused on that note to let the team soak it in, but we all knew where the conversation was leading.

"I think it's safe to say, if there are supernatural players in our banquet important enough to merit platinum membership, the scepter will be among their ranks, and it'll likely be in the most restricted area on the property. This fabled basement is large, it's private, and it's secured. It's where the silvans will meet with the mark, where the scepter will make an appearance, and where we plan to strike."

The Plan

The statement warranted a moment of grim silence. A month ago, this plan would've been crazy. While the team was familiar with hellions, due to my abilities, we generally hadn't encountered them as obstacles. This was quickly changing.

Bedrock, of course, was our demonic boss, the one who blackmailed each of us into servitude. Or, for some, just a liminal boss who paid well. I wasn't privy to why the Wire and the Lead were on the team. I didn't know how much each owed or was getting paid. These details were the domain of the Custodian, and it was only just recently that I learned what he really was.

I'd also encountered demons in the wild playing for other teams. These collective revelations had opened my eyes to all sorts of things playing in our world, and not just wizards and hellions. I'd known the others existed, I'd read up on them and summoned them, but I'd always been under the impression that there were rules to be followed. Laws to be obeyed.

But if there's one thing I learned the last couple of weeks, it's that anytime a rule exists, those affected by the rule will do anything and everything they can to maneuver around it.

Strolling into the Puzzle Box had been a big escalation for the team. It meant they were in the big leagues right alongside me. I also feared it meant the Custodian was out of control. As his secrets were unraveled, it only emboldened him more. Here he was, calmly organizing our next score, ostensibly at the behest of Bedrock, but to what end?

As usual, I got through these things by focusing on the job at hand.

"So," asked the Wire, eager to start, "where do you need me?"

The Custodian lowered his phone. "The Conway House has no indoor cameras, partially to preserve its historic integrity, but mostly to preserve the integrity of those within. Still, we can be sure other means of security will be heavy. Helping Home contracted Lock-E for the event, so we know they're serious."

Cisco's brow furrowed at the reference, and the Wire explained. "They're a high-level security company that caters to the elite. They're armed, they're experienced, and they have expensive toys. But I have a contact within their ranks. I'll get what I can."

The Custodian nodded and moved on to the Lead. "For you, I'm in the process of securing gold patron access.

Under your alias, you'll get us past the gate. I'm not sure if that includes the Wire or not, depending what he digs up. As for your role, you'll be an entertaining guest who cares passionately about everyone having a home. You may need to distract a guard or tease some information or access from a fellow patron, and you won't be able to do so unless people believe you're connected and important."

"I know how to act the part," she said firmly.

"I'll supply the ID and membership paperwork, as well as back access accounts. Which brings us to the crux of the matter." He winked at me. "The Handler will sneak into the private lounge, find the basement, and lift the scepter."

"That's all, huh?" I chuckled harshly. "That plan sounds a little generic, don't you think?"

"That's because we don't have concrete information on the operation yet. I expect the addition of the Shadow will solve many of our problems." He eyed the necromancer. "Shadow magic is an interesting discipline. I assume it facilitates sneaking and hiding?"

"You assume right," said Cisco.

"Perfect. You'll back up the Handler. Stick with her every step of the way. Do what she says. As far as you're concerned, she's your boss. Do you have a problem with that?"

He shrugged and presented a wry smile to the group. "That's why I'm here."

I tried my best not to mug at him, but it came out anyway. All fun aside, the Custodian's meaning was clear. The last thing he wanted was Cisco going off script, off on his own vendetta, even if it was unavoidable to some extent. If he was with me, I was expected to babysit.

"It's not much," admitted the Custodian about the tentative plan, "and we only have a couple of days to smooth out the rough edges."

"The entire thing is rough edges," I said.

"Which means we better get to work. Wire, learn everything you can about the team scheduled for that night and the measures they'll have in place. Lead, familiarize yourself with your cover, the cause, and related associations." He used his phone to swipe files over to her. "You'll have more specifics incoming. In the meantime, I have some donor credentials to manufacture. I'll coordinate as information develops."

"Homework," chimed Cisco, one hand raised to the air like a pestering student. "Do I get some too?"

"Indeed, but first"—he turned to the Wire and the Lead—"you two are dismissed. I want an update in the next hour."

They glanced at each other and stood.

I sprang from my chair. "Aren't you gonna go with them?"

"I still need to disburse your assignments. That will be a longer conversation. No need to hold them up. We're on a tight schedule."

I swallowed and followed them to the door to see them out, a pit growing in my stomach at the thought of being left alone with the Custodian. Without them, there might be no need for the charade. Without the charade, we'd need to face the music. I couldn't think of a way to stall them that would actually work, and Cisco didn't seem at all concerned.

The door shut. The Custodian dropped his head and cleared his throat. When he lifted his chin, he looked directly at Cisco. There were no overt actions, no threats, but his supreme confidence was enough to get the point across. He and Cisco converged on each other. Bernard warily skirted to the edge of the room, with me watching opposite.

"I've been open with you," stated the Custodian coolly. "Now it's time to reciprocate. What exactly is your interest in the convocation?"

I dreaded the smart-aleck remark coming in return, but everyone seemed invested in preserving the peace. Cisco found it within himself to hold back.

"I have a score to settle with the silvans," he disclosed. "A few of them tried to off me at their wedding a little while ago, and I know how to hold a grudge."

That doubtless sparked a flurry of ideas in the Custodian's head, but his opinions were indecipherable on the outside. After a tense moment, my boss nodded in acceptance. "Understandable. As long as we're not at cross purposes, I don't see any reason we can't help each other. Just keep in mind that you're on the team now. Your conduct reflects on the Handler, on *Shyla*. Remember that."

Cisco glanced my way, surprised my boss had used my real name. It was an implicit threat that he could get to me, that blowing the score would have real consequences.

"That won't be a problem," replied the animist.

And there it was. The Custodian didn't care if Cisco got what he wanted, as long as it didn't interfere with what he wanted. Honor among thieves.

"Homework, then," he pronounced.

"This oughta be good," said Cisco.

"I wouldn't classify it as good, but it's weighty. Part of the reason I dismissed the rest of the team is because we're flying more blind than usual."

I arched an eyebrow. "You don't want them to know how little we know."

"I don't want to bother them with the concern. They're treading in water higher than any they've ever known. It'll be up to us to reassure them. We're going to get the information we need before the job starts by doing a little legwork. And with the inclusion of the Shadow, we have an extra pair of legs. So let's start, shall we?"

Cisco and I traded a glance and paid attention.

The Custodian went back to his phone and sent me a new file. "The first page of this spreadsheet lists all Helping Home gold patrons. The next page whittles that list down to everyone within fifty miles, including many that are temporarily in town."

"You're recreating the guest list," I surmised.

"As near as I can. There's a high degree of certainty that the majority on the trimmed list have RSVPed to the banquet. The methodology, however, has flaws. For anyone visiting from out of town, it's a safe assumption they're here for the banquet, but for those already living locally, their presence merely indicates the possibility of attendance, but not their intent. For this reason, and for added anonymity, my thinking is we target out-of-towners."

He slipped his phone into the pocket of his slacks. "Conway Junior, for example. He's been a local celebrity his entire life. He manages the trust that owns the Conway House. But the man hasn't made a public appearance in years. He's bedridden at his current residence. Speculation about how his fortune will be distributed upon his looming death has been the subject of countless gossip rags. I think it's safe to say he's not on the guest list."

"Okay," I said. "Why are we interested in actual guests?"

"Because within the last hour I encountered a rumor of a pass token that admits entry to the charity function. Think of it like a golden ticket, except it's something substantial, handmade just for this event."

"And we don't have a pass token," guessed Cisco.

The Custodian shook his head. "I can manipulate the paperwork to give the Lead valid credentials and put her on the official guest list, but without a physical pass token, she'll be dead in the water."

"So you want us to snatch one from an attending guest."

"Which leads us to the opposite problem," he said. "Anyone who has a token has already RSVPed and is planning to attend. A public theft of one will cast suspicion on any unknowns entering the banquet."

"So we have two days to change someone's mind about attending the premier shindig of the month," mused Cisco. "Piece of cake."

"I'll leave that to you two," returned the Custodian. "On

top of that, there's the usual legwork."

"Casing the target," I said.

"Yes. It will be useful to get eyes on the grounds before the event. Any intelligence we gather will go a long way. We don't even know where the entrance to the basement level is."

"Or if it exists," I muttered.

"Lastly, the Helping Home main office is only staffed three days out of the week. That makes today the last day of business before the charity event. It's a long shot, but it might be worth keeping an eye on them. In situations like this, opportunities often come where you least expect them."

Cisco grimaced. "Sounds like busywork to me."

I put my arm on his shoulder. "We'll get it done."

The Custodian appraised us a moment. "I'm sure you will. And it'll be a good chance for some operational experience before the big day."

He made for the door. I was so happy to see him go that I didn't stop him with any questions. When I shut the door, Bernard visibly relaxed. We'd both butted heads with the Custodian before so it was good to know he still needed us.

For now, at least.

Alone at Last

I breathed deeply, waiting with my back resting on the door, until I knew the Custodian was gone for good. I realized my eyes were closed and opened them to an inquisitive Cisco.

"This is the big bad master thief?" he asked with a chuckle. "What're you so nervous for?"

I glared at the idiot. "You are *so* lucky he wasn't interested in blowing his cover."

"Who, the Custodian?"

"Yes." I opened the door and checked the hall before locking up again. I lowered my voice anyway. "He isn't what he seems." I went for the kitchen to top off my coffee. The resultant mixture wasn't hot enough, so I nuked it in the microwave for thirty seconds.

"That's gross," said Cisco. "Trust me, I know coffee."

I rolled my eyes. "Why don't you tell me what you *don't* know? That'll be quicker, apparently."

He snorted, and I wasn't altogether sure whether he had

taken the statement as a compliment or an insult. He joined me in the kitchen and emptied the pot into his mug. "Look, don't do this thing that women always do. Just tell me what you mean."

"Women, huh? You projecting much?"

"Leave Milena out of this. It's a tough time for her. She was practically dead."

"Fine, then don't treat me like some basic bitch starting arguments for fun. You're the one that's a stereotype. You walk into a room and somehow always find yourself at its center."

He smiled. "Now who's projecting?"

I scoffed. "It is just like you to suggest I have a thing for you, like I can't help but swoon at a well-tanned man in a muscle shirt."

He sipped his coffee in amusement and flexed his triceps. "So you noticed my muscles."

"Please. I wouldn't dream of touching you."

"Shyla, I hate to break it to you, but you're a little old for me."

My eyes flared. "Mentally, no doubt."

Bernard very loudly and very intentionally cleared his throat. We slowly turned to the gargoyle sitting on his haunches at the edge of the kitchen. I swallowed my anger, embarrassed.

Cisco backed up a step, leaned against the kitchen island, and scratched his neck. "Wow, he really is like a dog, isn't he? You just forget he's there."

"I've lived for a thousand years, mortal," chided the

gargoyle. "You'd do well not to forget about me."

Cisco canted his head in silent concession of the point. I pulled my coffee from the microwave. It was a little too hot and I slammed the door a little too loudly.

Cisco noticed my evident frustration. He sighed and took a sip from his mug and regarded me thoughtfully. "Look," he finally said, "I'm a wrecking ball. I know that. It's why the monsters hate me."

I smirked. "If you're trying to apologize, you're doing an awful job."

He laughed and I did too. "Okay, fine. So tell me what you mean about this Custodian guy. He one of those connected mafia types? Because I know the type."

"Oh, he's connected," I said with a snort, "but he might be closer to those monsters you're talking about."

"You're saying he isn't human? I didn't get that impression."

"That's because he's very good at what he does. I worked closely with him for nine years before ever getting a whiff of his true nature. He's been against me the whole time. He's the whole reason..."

I didn't finish the sentence. Cisco didn't need to know my sob story. My father trapped in Hell, Asmodeus in the guise of Bedrock, feigning to be my boss, and the Custodian, the true power in the whole depraved operation.

My voice came back, soft and somber. "The Custodian's identity is his biggest secret. It's both his strength and his weakness. He might kill me just for telling you. Or he might kill you."

The animist watched me solemnly, clenching his jaw but perhaps not as cocky.

"You want a peek into my world?" I challenged. "Into my kinds of problems? They're not for the faint of heart, Cisco."

He nodded. "I've had a fair amount of that business myself."

Not like this, I thought, but I didn't want to keep objecting. I'd already drawn the conversation far enough along that I couldn't turn it around. Cisco was here, he wanted to know, and maybe, just maybe, he could help me just as I help him.

"What is he, Shyla?" he asked softly.

I blew into my mug and took a sip, finally getting the temp down to something reasonable. I savored the flavor for a long moment before setting it down.

"Okay," I said, "I'm going to trust you because you're a big boy. But I need you to trust me in turn. Trust that when I tell you he's dangerous, you don't shrug it off with a schlocky comeback. You need to believe me no matter how much of a tough guy you are. Got it?"

His face was appropriately sober. "Fine."

And he meant it.

"There's no easy way to say this," I told him, "but the Custodian is an angel."

His eyes narrowed. "Like..."

"A real angel. His name's Abaddon, the Angel of the Abyss mentioned in *Revelation*. He's the Lord of the Pit, residing in the eighth ring of Hell."

Cisco frowned, ticked his fingers, and then set his mug down to continue on the second hand. "That would be..."

I rolled my eyes. "The Malebolge. We're talking the abandoned, wild reaches of Hell before the relative civilization of Pandemonium."

His face was a jumble of incomprehension and skepticism, and he had taken the news just about as well as I could imagine anyone doing. "Is... Is he some type of guardian or watcher or something?"

"Not a watcher. That word's reserved for a class of fallen angels in the *Book of Enoch*. Abaddon's a full-on angel, except he's not one of the good guys."

Cisco frowned. "I'm not sure any of them are, really."

My eyes fixed on him before my face sagged in exhausted denial. "No. No way. You're not about to tell me you've met angels before too."

He shrugged sheepishly. "I'm not sure. I don't wanna come off as a cocksure know-it-all."

"Stop it. Do you know any other angels or what?"

"I've met one a couple times before. To be honest, I wasn't too impressed."

"In their prowess?"

"What do you think I am, stupid? I didn't say I fought one." He sipped his coffee.

"Then what?"

"I don't know. Seemed an all right guy. Gave me good advice once. But when I really needed his help, he didn't bother to lift a finger. It was like talking to a brick wall."

I blinked at him, surprised by his wealth of experience.

Maybe the thought of him helping me wasn't a desperate gambit after all. I entertained the possibility of speaking to another angel, someone with power who wasn't so closely aligned with Abaddon. Maybe there was a strategy in there. A way out of my prison.

"That makes a little sense," I said. "Believe it or not, I don't have much experience with angels, but it's a summoner's business to extensively research apocrypha, grimoires, the Bible, and various exegeses. From everything I know and have heard, angels are powerful but have great limits imposed upon them. They're supposed to lead without acting."

"Creatures of guidance," mused Cisco. "That's what Malik told me they were."

My eyes widened slightly. "Malik?"

"Yeah, that's my Celestial buddy. You know him?"

"Only by reputation. Not a lot's written about him. In fact, he's not in any Christian or Jewish texts. In the Quran, he's said to be the angel who administers the hellfire."

Cisco groaned. "Another angel of the abyss then?"

"It's possible, but Hell has an open-door policy. Who knows where Malik spends the brunt of his time?"

"The Aether and the Nether, as far as I know."

"That makes sense," I said after thinking about it. "I always thought angels, like hellions, weren't allowed on Earth except for special cases. The Elemental Planes are a workaround of sorts."

"Wait a minute. You're telling me the Celestials are using legal loopholes?"

I snickered and went for my coffee mug again. "In the business of Heaven and Hell, it happens much more than you might think."

He finished his coffee with a gulp and set the empty in the sink. "I just had a troubling thought. What if this is the reason to hold the convocation on Earth? No angelic interference?" His brow furrowed. "Wait a minute. If that's true, how's Abaddon running around planning elaborate heists? Are you saying he's on official business?"

I exhaled. "Actually, my guess is the opposite. It's complicated, but Abaddon holds the Ring of Solomon. It's a powerful relic that elevates him even higher above our weight class than he already is. The Ring commands demons which, like all summoning, bends the rules by harboring foreign actors in the Material Plane. The best I can figure is the Ring allows an exception to the rule. Abaddon's found the ultimate loophole."

"Clever guy." Cisco went to the wall of windows and stared at the clear sky for a bit. "Maybe we can use Abaddon's connections to our advantage." He turned to me with a grin. "He knows Hell, right? He's the Lord of the Pit, which apparently isn't just a badass *Magic: The Gathering* card." He lifted his hand and signaled ironic devil horns with an upraised index finger and pinkie.

Cisco had moved beyond the heist. He was thinking of his stiges again, the reason he tracked my silvan messenger into the Puzzle Box in the first place. I found it curious. We were both animists but could hardly be more different, each with separate motivations to be in the underground that night. Yet our disparate missions didn't just cross paths, they shared the road together.

It could've all been an elaborate coincidence, but I tended not to believe in such things.

"That's a big risk," I hedged. "We can't just ask Abaddon about the stiges. If we do and he has any investment in them at all, he'd work against us and keep us in the dark. A single mention could blow the whole investigation. No, your explanation of personal payback is something he can understand. It also isn't a threat to him. We bring up the stiges, it might alter your value proposition."

"That's a funny way to put him killing me," he said sourly. "Okay, I get it. This one's your call. You know the guy more than I do."

I appreciated that. Cisco wore the disappointment plainly on his face, but he trusted me. For a split second I had the glimmer of hope that we could work together without royally screwing everything up.

Just for a split second.

Hey, I wasn't convinced about the guy. He was formidable but, like he'd said, he was a wrecking ball. The types of jobs my crew went for usually required a little more finesse.

"I know someone we can ask," I said as a peace offering, "but we better do it with Milena around. We want to ask about her too."

His face brightened. "Great, I'll go get her."

"Let's do it tonight. The convocation's coming up and we need to get moving on our preparations. We have jobs, remember."

"I do." He stood straighter. "Do we have any idea why the Custodian wants this particular piece of treasure?"

"What do you mean?" I asked. "It's what we do."

"I mean this particular heist, given the nonhuman element, seems a little hairy. I don't buy your angel being motivated by a big payday."

I grunted. He might be right.

Cisco clapped his hands together. "All right. Pick a name from your list, send me there, and I'll come back with your pass token."

"Not so fast, Rambo. You're not getting the pass token. I want you watching the Helping Home office. It's easy to get there from here."

His eyes fluttered. "You're kidding me. That's worse than busywork. It's a waste of time."

"And yet it needs to be done. Make an afternoon of it. I'm the boss, remember?"

He stared. "Are you serious?"

"Hey, you're the one who wanted to work with me. You want it done without payment. Let's do what it takes."

My eyes must've sparkled because he relented with a gruff nod. "Whatever you say."

I jotted down the address on a sticky note and handed it to him. He took it begrudgingly, making his objection known several times over with actions instead of words. In some ways he was a big baby.

"We'll do my thing tonight then," he said. "And don't try to flake on me." He winked. "I know where you live."

I replied with a snide cock of my head. "No worries on that end, Cisco. You're in this deep now. Deeper than you know."

Homework

Bernard trailed behind me as I retrieved my personal phone from the bedroom.

"You think it's wise to tell him so much?" he asked. "I can see his appeal, but necromancers aren't known for being trustworthy."

"Remind me again what people think of demon summoners?"

I plopped onto the side of my bed and pulled on riding boots as I dialed my neighbor from two floors down.

"Besides, I never said I trusted him."

Josalie picked up after three rings. "Hey girl!" she chimed, voice light and sunny. "What a relief to hear from you."

"Oh yeah? Why's that?"

"Ugh." She sighed dramatically. "The kids are with grandma at Graciela's. Marlon and I finally have the house alone but he's too tired to rock my world. I'm sexually frustrated over here."

I laughed. "I don't think I can help you with that, but I might have the next best thing."

"Please. Anything."

"You know how you're always asking to join the crew and do cool stuff? I might have a job for you."

"What are we gonna do?" she asked excitedly. "Hot-wire a Lambo? Rob a bank? Lay it on me, girl."

"My life isn't a spy movie, Jo, but I do want you to do a little surveillance. Go to the bar downstairs and watch a couple of people for me. You can't miss the guy. He thinks he's all that and walks around in red cowboy boots. His girlfriend's something else too. You'll see what I mean."

"Hmm," she pondered, slightly skeptical but no less excited. "It doesn't sound like a lot of intrigue to me."

"I just want you to see what they're up to. Maybe you overhear their plans. And you can order anything you want. The tab's on me."

"You know that's right! You got yourself a deal, homie." She was so happy to get out of the house that she hung up before I could explain more. Maybe that was for the best, considering everything about my life she didn't know.

Bernard chuckled. "You're cold as ice, Shyla." His statement was said in an approving tone. "You've really thought of everything, haven't you?"

"One can never be too careful. And speaking of which..."

I made my way around the bed to the large wardrobe. I revealed the standing mirror inside by pulling away the silk bathrobe draped over it.

"Knock, knock," I said, tapping the glass. "Anyone

home?"

I waited a moment but Asmodeus didn't answer. It wasn't the usual midnight rendezvous time so reaching him wasn't guaranteed. Which was too bad. The hellion, like me, was under Abaddon's thumb. While it was against his commands to directly disobey the angel, it was always possible to squeeze some information from him. Like why this scepter was so important, for example.

But I could always get the info later. I covered the mirror and shut the wardrobe. I did a few minutes of research on my phone before I was content to head out. I unsummoned Bernard, pocketed both cell phones, and locked up.

I called Trap from the hallway.

"Hey there," came his smooth-as-butter voice. "How is my favorite demon-summoning cat burglar today?"

I rolled my eyes. "You sure know how to make a girl feel special. I need you to do some background for me."

"What are you into this time?"

"Got eyes on a charity function at the Conway House. I was surprised to see the Conway heir listed as a Helping Home patron."

"Shyla, the man's probably on the donor lists of every registered non-profit in the hemisphere."

"I know, but something about this one bugs me. The banquet seems too important to go unnoticed. I'm gonna check it out. I'd like you to look into it on your end, too. Anything about Conway, the property, and Helping Home."

"Piece of cake," he said.

"There's another thing. Apparently Helping Home publishes their list of gold patrons, but there's a secret platinum tier. I need a list. Even one name can help."

"That sounds like a challenge. I'm on it."

"And Trap? Don't dig too invasively. This one's touchy business and I don't want your fingerprints all over it for anyone to find, least of all my boss. It goes without saying I'm not supposed to bring you in on this."

"Always. And no worries. I'll be a ghost."

"Thanks, Trap."

I clicked him off just as the elevator opened. In a minute I was exiting the parking garage on the Ducati Monster, L-Twin engine rumbling as I pulled to the corner beside the brunch bar at the bottom floor of my building. A glance through the wide windows showed Cisco and Milena chatting at the bar as Josalie arrived. She planted her butt at the other end of the bar and ordered a beer.

The game was afoot.

I flicked my Corse Carbon helmet closed and sped off in the other direction.

Although the famous Conway House was an old mansion in the hills, there was time for it later. Casing a place like that properly would require the cover of night. For now I was hoping to be a bit more straightforward with some good old-fashioned boots on the ground.

After a pleasant ride, I pulled to the curb of a serene street in an old mid-city neighborhood. Trees towered on either side, meeting at the middle and casting a comfortable gloom over the day. The current residence of John Conway

Jr. was decidedly more modest than the hill house. Its two stories sat upright and square at the end of a long front lawn. Oblong windows were lined with foliage, and a towering cactus edged out the house as the tallest thing on the property.

I set my helmet and gloves aside and strode up the walkway, tussling my hair so it fell naturally over my shoulders. I realized to my chagrin that I still had the Grateful Dead tee on, so I kept my black leather jacket zipped and stepped onto the small porch. Affixed to the frame atop the heavy white door was a metal cross. As far as first impressions went, it was a start. There was a camera in the corner of the ceiling. I knocked.

I didn't hear anything for a bit, but just as I knocked again there was some movement through the window. Just a changing of light. Someone shuffled to and opened the door. It was a handsome man in his forties or fifties. He wore a suit and had dashes of gray in his black hair over his ears. Since he was way too young to be John Conway I assumed he was a butler.

"Hi," I said as pleasantly as I could. "My name is Wanda Evans. I'm with Helping Home and I was hoping to see Mr. Conway, please." Smiles didn't come naturally to me but I made an effort.

Unfortunately, charm only went so far. The trim man ran his eyes over me like he was appraising a race horse and grunted imperceptibly. "I'm not aware of any appointments today."

"Yes, I'm sorry. We spoke a few weeks ago in regards to

the House and something came up at the last second. I was hoping we could clear it up without an appointment."

The man pressed his lips together and waited, as if he had said all he intended to. It was a risk, but I took the chance to assure him further.

"If you like, you can ring the Helping Home office and ask about me." I laughed congenially. "So you don't think I'm some burglar." I realized I didn't have the phone number at the tip of my tongue. How bad would it be if I had to look it up in front of him?

He allowed a hint of a smile. "No, ma'am, that won't be necessary. I'll take you at your word. Unfortunately, without a due appointment, it will be impossible to see Mr. Conway today."

I opened my mouth for another round of negotiation but the door shut in my face. Two locks clicked and the man scuttled away.

I stepped off the porch and huffed. Even when I tried to be straightforward I had to resort to subterfuge. I walked across the lawn, past windows with drawn curtains, and made for the backyard. At this rate, I wasn't likely to get inside, but I could do a minute of snooping before I moved on.

I hopped an iron gate onto a brick patio. A Roman pool was set into the first half of the yard, with manicured grass and a line of bushes along the back fence. I eyeballed another security camera on the wall of the house and hurried under it into what looked to be a blind spot. I peeked into a dining room window. The table was bare and the chairs were perfectly spaced, as if the room was little used. I was about to dash to the next window when the back door opened. I turned to retreat.

The butler cleared his throat. "Excuse me, Ms. Crowe."

I froze and slowly swiveled around. The man wore an unamused expression even more plain than his suit. I straightened and watched him carefully, struggling to come up with a story.

"Mr. Conway will see you now."

Death's Door

I brushed my hair to one side in an attempt to appear dignified and nodded sheepishly. "Okay... Great."

Amply embarrassed, I followed him inside without word. He waited by the back door to close it after me, which left me a little on edge, but apparently it was only a formality. He once again took the lead through the house. The furniture was well-used, and there were a lot of knickknacks collected on every shelf and corner. The home was neatly kept but had obviously seen its fair share of living. It had a warm quality to it, or maybe it was more accurate to say it used to. I couldn't shake the feeling that it was now abandoned. It reminded me of leafing through pictures of Chernobyl apartments.

We went up the staircase and to the master bedroom, where the butler announced me and held the door open. I stepped in and was a little stunned to see a man far past his prime in an adjustable hospital bed.

Stunned but not entirely surprised. John Conway might

not have been at death's door, but he was on the stoop.

The old philanthropist had an oxygen mask at his side and a slew of machines for monitoring his condition and offering care. An IV slow dripped medication, likely to mitigate the pain. John was weak but percipient for his ninety-six years. He nodded at the door and the butler took his leave, shutting it behind him and retiring down the stairs. The old man watched on a series of monitors at his bedside. Among other video feeds, he had a clear view of the front porch and the backyard.

"Mr. Conway," I said.

"Ms. Crowe. Shall we now dispense with the formalities?"

His voice was strong coming from such a frail body. It conveyed the iron will I assumed a man like him must have. At that moment old age seemed a curse that neither endless money nor stalwart determination could stave off.

"Of course," I answered.

"Good. You wanted to see me, Shyla?"

I swallowed. I was unsettled when older men knew my business. Force of habit. "How do you know me?"

"Oh, it's my business to know of such people." His smile carried only a hint of smugness.

"What people?" I asked.

"Are we really going to continue this masquerade? Old men like me don't have time for pretense. Not unless they have grandchildren to play it with, and I've long ago diverged from that path."

Everyone in the city knew Conway's history. His wife

had died young and he never remarried or had kids. The story was similar to his father's, except it was a young mother who died and left behind a son. Now, the proper family line would end with a whimper in this room, which might've been why the old man gave so much of his money away.

I nodded. "Okay, John."

He smiled amicably. "Your services are for hire in the city," he said, "and you do your job well. If it wasn't for people like me knowing about people like you, no one would get any business done."

John Conway had a sterling reputation for being smart and kind. Five seconds in and he was living up to expectations. He lifted a hand and beckoned me closer.

"Come. Let me get a look at you."

I acquiesced, taking the opportunity to study his security monitors. The butler was preparing a meal in the kitchen, and the property was otherwise empty. "I guess you know I'm not from Helping Home then."

"No, but you're right to be interested in them."

"Am I?"

"Of course. They're not on the side of the angels."

I could only respond with half a smile. "And you are?"

Once again, "Of course."

I crossed my arms and swung my weight to one hip. "Wanna tell me about them?"

The old man gazed into a distant past and sighed. "The Conway House, in some ways, is our family's greatest legacy. Not the brick and mortar, mind you. Not even the property itself, but what it represents. My family developed those hills. You could say we had a hand in creating this town. And very soon we'll be leaving it all behind."

I wasn't sure if he meant the House or the city. The distinction didn't seem to matter.

"My vast fortune too," he added sourly, "which I'm sure you've already looked into."

I stayed mum about what I did and didn't know. Expectations worked both ways, and he saw me as a professional.

The old man tried to lean forward, but he could only manage a dip of his head. "But what good is money to me now? I have no sons or daughters. And I've long ago learned that most charities exist to line the pockets of the charitable. Even when they coalesce from high-minded goals, it only takes a hint of greed to redirect all their potential for good." He grunted. "Like people, the longer an organization lives, the easier it is to corrupt."

"Are you referring to Helping Home or yourself?"

He chuckled oddly, seemingly amused at being spoken to like that. With his fame and power, the man had very few detractors. "I've certainly had my temptations, Shyla. But then, I also have a guardian angel."

I furrowed my brow, unsure of his meaning yet again.

John's eyes searched mine a moment, and then he made his move. "Be direct with an old man. Allow me that concession. You deal outside the normal jurisdiction of humanity, do you not?"

It was a tense moment. I was rarely so forward with

strangers about my occupation, but the combination of John's frail body and good nature compelled me to play along with a faint nod. "That's why I'm here."

"In regards to?"

"Helping Home platinum patrons."

His eyes brightened. "So you are aware. Like you, they also have ties outside the human realm." He sighed. "You know, there was a time I could've bought that charity outright ten times over. Now they don't even admit to the fact that the platinum level exists."

I was pretty sure where he was going with this but didn't want to be caught flat-footed. Innuendo made for sexy dialog, but it tended toward the impractical. "You don't like Helping Home very much, do you, John?"

"Ah, a fellow admirer of candor. No, I do not like them. They may have been altruistic once, but now they're a vile organization. Their presence defaces our world. They wish to use what I have built for nefarious gain, and I'll do what I can to prevent it. That's why I invited you in."

I pulled away from him, surprised. "You want to hire me? But how did you know... ?"

"I didn't know you were coming, Shyla, but I knew someone would. I have a feeling about these things." He studied me a moment. "I have a feeling for people too. Call it... my gift."

I casually searched the room for signs of spellcraft.

"You're a thief," he said flatly. "I know that. But you're also on the side of good. Tell me I'm wrong."

My head gave a hesitant half shake before stopping on

the thought. I wasn't sure how to answer that question. For my entire life, I'd been raised to take advantage of those with greater means and fewer smarts. I wasn't an evil bastard like Abaddon or Asmodeus, but I never would've described myself as resting on the opposite side of that scale.

"Do you have a guardian angel too?" he pried. "A real angel?"

If he only knew the half of it. "John... I don't think..."

He pointed at my chest. "You're wearing a pentacle. May I see it?"

The observation startled me. The only thing visible on my neckline was the black leather cord. I unzipped the jacket a smidge and pulled out the Sigillum Dei. It was a weighty gold amulet. After recent events had proven its utility in defense, I'd lengthened the cord it hung on. This allowed the amulet a greater range of motion, though I still had to lean toward the bed for the old man to see it.

"The Seal of God," he whispered with reverence. His hand came up to clasp it, and I fought the urge to recoil. He cupped it gingerly and the amulet let off faint light, as if the gold was reflecting the light of the sun.

He nodded in satisfaction. "We are warriors, Shyla, you and I. We do what needs to be done to perpetuate good."

I drew away, taking the pentacle with me. Its warmth immediately faded. "Sorry, you've got the wrong girl."

"I don't believe I do. Why else would you come to me, in my moment of need?"

He signaled to a desk in the corner. I had scanned it before and didn't see anything worthwhile. But then my eyes landed on what I'd thought to be a small paperweight. A brass bell, though not a real one. It rested on its side and had a flat back like a Christmas ornament.

My eyes widened. "The pass token for the banquet."

"Right you are," he chirped approvingly. "You want to get into that party, don't you?"

I went to the desk and tested the weight of the ornament. On the flat underside was an inscription of John's name. That was a slight complication, though easy enough to correct.

"You must know what I built on that estate," he said, voice growing colder. "My man can fill you in on the finer points of entering the basement parlor, but you must first understand what is down there."

I returned to the bedside and listened raptly.

"When you make your way through the underground, the first thing you lose is yourself. You must become a nameless individual among other nameless individuals. You then travel through the dark in absolute silence, your mind stripped to its purest essence. Next, your soul will be laid bare by the very light of God Himself. It is only after you emerge from these trials that you will reach the divination chamber."

He was pouring on the ceremony a little heavy, but I didn't interrupt.

"My father built a divinity gate, Shyla. It's a powerful circle that can be used for summoning and accessing forbidden knowledge, among other things. It possesses a connection to demons as well as angels, and possibly other beings that would terrify even them. It's a doorway, and it must be destroyed."

Great, the old man ditched the ceremony and went straight for the jugular. I had to admit, even accounting for a healthy dose of exaggeration, I didn't like the sound of this thing. I also found the similarity and dichotomy of the two words curious. Divination and divinity had the same root, but they meant two very different things. The first was the search for answers from beyond, while the second was a reference to the one doing the answering.

"If you can do this thing," John said, "destroy the gate, rectify our family's greatest mistake, you will earn the gratitude of a dying man. Gratitude, alongside half a million dollars."

My lashes flared. That kind of money would buy off two months from the Custodian. It would keep my ledger in the black.

"Do you know anything about who's attending the banquet?" I asked. "About a scepter?"

He tiredly shook his head. "I know of no details. Study is difficult from this bed of mine. I don't even know who the platinum patrons are."

"Silvans."

"Bah, some of them no doubt, but there are forces at play much worse than those Earthly aberrations. Their plans are as obscure as their identities. One thing is clear: my estate stands to destroy the world as we know it."

His breathing quickened and grew more labored. Not only was he unnecessarily excitable, but the normally benign man was starting to sound a little tattered around the edges. A little desperate.

"Battle lines are being drawn, young lady."

His voice trembled. One of his machines beeped and began reporting a heightened heart rate.

"It's okay," I soothed. "Just take it easy."

His expression intensified. "You're the one to stop it, Shyla Crowe. You're the one that must fight the good fight in my stead."

I shuffled nervously and glanced around the empty room. The butler wasn't on any of the video screens.

"What are you talking about, John?"

He leaned into me, this time lurching his bent body forward with crazed eyes. "I'm talking about nothing other than Hell on Earth."

Fresh Air

I left the residence looking over my shoulder, eyeing the cross above the doorway on the porch. So much for good vibes. What had begun as a bit of snooping had totally unnerved me.

In my line of work, it wasn't uncommon to encounter true believers. Coming face-to-face with supreme beings spawns overzealous and overactive imaginations. John Conway's particular brand bordered on madness.

It wasn't that I didn't believe in angels, obviously. I just didn't buy the fate of the world being at stake. Humankind has been around for thousands of years. It's the height of arrogance to believe our lives, above all others, warrant the end times.

Even more cocky was thinking we could do something about it.

I returned to the familiar comfort of the Ducati's padded seat, armoring myself with gloves and helmet and resolve, and riding fast to relax my nerves.

Everything said, the affair had been an undeniable success. The butler gave me the lay of the Conway House, I acquired the brass ornament, and I was offered a new score to boot. Not a bad thirty minutes of work.

But I had questions after hearing what amounted to juicy gossip. I didn't fully comprehend the danger of Conway's summoning circle. I myself had a custom one in my loft for personal use. Sure, the one in the Conway House purportedly summoned angels, but that didn't sound so terrible.

Not to say I was a naive sentimentalist. I, more than anybody, knew of an angel's potential for wickedness. It was more that I had confidence in their capabilities. Celestials didn't seem the type to be easily taken advantage of, let alone summoned.

Then there was the talk of a guardian angel. I didn't know what John Conway believed, but I had the Lord of the Pit breathing down my neck, holding the Ring of Solomon and the life of my father over my head.

So was this a rock and a hard place, or was it a problem and an opportunity? With the powers set against me being so great, wasn't it only fair I had an angel in my corner to even the odds? The possibilities were staggering.

The only thing I knew for sure was that John Conway wanted the divinity gate destroyed if it was the last thing he did with his life.

I had gotten so much done in so little time that I decided to utilize my momentum. I found myself driving into the hills and heading for the Conway House. The Monster's engine echoed off the sheer rock face on the road's edge as I wound through the sloping streets. They narrowed at points, but the residential roads plateaued at the mountaintop. Sun beating down with the breeze in my face, I roared past a picturesque water reservoir. The natural landscape was fenced off from the general public, but it provided a beautiful view.

The neighborhood was a hidden gem, flatter and more spacious than the properties at lower elevations. The old estate occupied prime real estate. It might've been the first built in the area.

A high stone wall fronted the property for a long block before the gate came into view. It was old wrought iron, blanketed with neatly clipped vines that obscured the view inside. I rolled on by with the throttle low. There were no cars parked for another block until the next residence, and no pedestrians in sight. I continued down the road a minute before flipping around and approaching again. All quiet on the home front.

I had an incoming call on my personal phone so I parked across the street and twenty feet down from the gate and pulled off my helmet.

"Trap," I answered, holding the cell with my shoulder as I peeled a glove off. "How's things?"

"Slow and steady," he returned. "I did some digging into the players. Most of the Conway family saga is well known by now so I focused on Helping Home. They're a growing charity across several states but still fairly new in the scheme of things. They were founded fifteen years ago. When they found success after the housing crash, their executive director died under mysterious circumstances. Drove straight off a cliff in the middle of the desert. Foul play was rumored but never taken into serious consideration."

"You think someone moved in on their operation?"

"It's hard to prove but it's a definite possibility. After that, the org enjoyed wider success and expansion, but again, most attribute that to the timing with the recession. And then there's the fact that the directors who followed weren't exactly evil dictator types. Each has been a known figure in the public service sector, and each only served a few years until surrendering the role to their successor. Helping Home is currently on their sixth executive director, one Jamala Trebierre. I poked into her past but she seems as benign as they come."

"Okay," I said, working through the logic with him. "So they're pretty faces, hired for branding and legitimacy, with no real say in the long-term goals of the charity."

"Another solid assumption, but ultimately another dead end."

It was true we couldn't prove anything. Then again, my business wasn't exactly a court of law. I dealt in the margins, often making decisions based on rumor and speculation. I may have been a professional, but I was the furthest thing from legitimate my targets were apt to encounter. That's what made me dangerous.

"What about their finances?"

"This is the big one, but it's also going to be the toughest to crack. If this organization is a front of some kind, finding where the money goes answers all our questions. Problem is, finance law and the realities of international banking make it almost impossible to trace. On the surface, and even below it some ways, Helping Home is completely legitimate. They're taking in a whole lot of money, yes, but they appear to be spending it on their cause."

He took a breath to collect his thoughts. "All that's the bad news. We more or less expect some shady dealings, but we can't prove it. But I did find something curious when I cross-referenced Helping Home with the Conway trust. A sale is being expedited. The longstanding ownership of the Conway House is changing hands, and the new buyer is Helping Home."

I clicked my tongue. "That explains what the old man said about them taking everything he's built. They're forcing the sale on him."

"Wait," said Trap, cutting me off. "You saw the man himself? He's practically a hermit now."

"Not by choice. He's real sick and confined to his bed. Not to say he isn't his own kind of crazy. There's something going on in that famous basement of his, and it has a little to do with my particular skill set."

Silence hung over the line for a few seconds. "You're not talking about safe-cracking, are you?"

I let the question go unanswered. "What about patron tiers? Have you found anything about the platinums?"

He snorted. "It's just gold tier, Shyla. There's nothing else. Conway himself, who seems pretty invested in the charity, is a gold member. Are you sure your info is reliable?"

I grimaced. Somehow his lack of proof just solidified my worry even more. "Unfortunately. Okay, Trap. You'll get your usual drop. Thanks."

"No problem. Do me a favor and keep someone close to you on this one. Someone you trust more than that slimy boss of yours. I'm not a field guy, but I'll be on hand if you need me."

After I hung up, I stared at the phone a while. It was the afternoon so I wasn't about to sneak into a historic landmark. I hadn't even been able to manage two minutes into Conway's backyard before being seen. No, better to play things safe for now and not put the score at risk.

I texted Josalie to see how things were going on her end. Her reply was to the point.

"Cisco left on errand. Milena still here. Food is great. #AfternoonPancakes."

I grinned. At least someone was enjoying themselves.

This was what I wrestled with when Josalie asked me what was really going on. She was a loving wife, a doting mom, a hardworking nurse, and never went anywhere without a smile. Was I really gonna be the one to break it to her that the world wasn't all sunshine and rainbows?

The vine-covered gate buzzed as it sprang to life, sliding aside. I hurriedly fit the helmet over my head to disguise myself, opening up my map app to look like a biker pondering their route to the next landmark.

A pickup truck with a covered bed waited to exit as the

gate opened. It was white with the blue-and-yellow logo of the security company Lock-E. The driver wore a matching uniform.

I gave the situation casual notice while I perused my phone. As the truck pulled away, another uniformed security worker stood on the drive. It was a long walk up to the house so another truck was parked just within, meaning the front gate was being watched. The blond security guard stared at me as the gate closed. I didn't dare make a move until the vines once again obstructed my view.

Two days before the event and the security company was already locking the place down. That effectively shut down my current case of the property. I wasn't sure it was even worth returning at night.

We already knew the basics. What little more we could glean by hitting the property early was no longer worth the risk-versus-reward calculation. Better to fly blind than intentionally crash and burn.

Drinking Buddies

I stopped the bike at the corner of my building and idly glanced inside the cafe window, ready to head into the garage, only to do a double take.

Josalie and Milena sat across a table from each other guffawing like one of them had just told the funniest joke in the world. They clinked glasses and downed a pair of shots.

What in the world?

I headed underground and parked the bike before making my way up the steps and entering my favorite breakfast establishment. Josalie's eyes went wide as I stomped up to their table and crossed my arms.

"What is it about the word subtle that misled you?"

After a moment of mollified silence, they both snorted in laughter. I was not amused.

"Relax," said Milena, "it was pretty obvious she was snooping."

My neighbor smiled sheepishly. "Sorry if I let you

down."

"Screw that," returned a visibly drunk Milena. "This was the best accident ever. This chick is seriously cool. Tell Shyla that story about the sex tacos!"

I rolled my eyes. "I know about the sex tacos."

"Of course she does," agreed Jo. "My bestie knows everything about me." She flashed me a knowing look, making me feel guilty for keeping secrets.

I sighed. "Okay, I guess there's no more point in funding this operation. What's the damage?"

I retrieved the check and was staggered by the amount of alcohol consumption in a relatively short time. While Josalie could pound a few, I was more concerned with what Milena had gone through. It must've been a rough night for her. She disappeared into the bathroom while I took care of the check.

I didn't say much as we headed up the elevator together. The two of them giggled like a couple of high school girls who'd just gotten in trouble with their mom. I didn't like where I fit into that particular metaphor and overcompensated by remaining casually aloof. I figured Josalie usually had a lot of responsibilities on her plate. It was nice to see her forget about them for an afternoon.

Once in the loft I had the urge to open a bottle of wine and join the party, but I guess I couldn't shake that mom comparison. Like it or not, I was the responsible one right now. I passed out glasses of water and started some tea. As I often did, I felt the pang to reach for my record player before remembering my music collection was all digital now. The technology wasn't as tactile, and I missed the smell of vinyl in the sleeves, but it got the job done. A few swipes on my phone and the Wi-Fi speakers filled the space with the upbeat tempo of the Steve Miller Band.

"I'm not gonna lie," said Milena, stretching on the couch. "This place is nice. But you need to get some blackout curtains in here."

I could sympathize. My work often kept me up into the night hours, meaning sleep came in the daytime. The wall of windows was north facing so I didn't get a direct stream of sun inside, but there was plenty of light to go around.

"It's nothing a pillow over your head can't fix," I returned. "You want one?"

I went to grab one but she stopped me. "No, I'm not sleeping now. You crazy?" She sat up and grabbed her water glass. "Cisco's working with you now?"

I glanced at Josalie, worried about saying too much. Then again, I'd asked her to eavesdrop. I'd figured she might get little hints about things. Get introduced to my world slowly and comfortably, in case she changed her mind and wanted to back off. For now my neighbor seemed content with snooping through my stuff.

"Just an extra pair of eyes for now. We split up to cover more ground."

Milena shook her head wistfully. "He's like a dog with a bone."

I snickered and sat down beside her. "What about you?"

She stared at nothing in particular for a little too long. "What about me?"

I hiked a shoulder. "Don't you wanna track down what these silvans are up to? Find out what the stiges did to you?"

"I don't think I care," she said with a sigh.

"Of course you do. You don't want to find yourself in hock to higher powers. Trust me on that."

But the words seemed lost on her. It was dumb of me to bring my own experiences into the conversation. I didn't know what she was dealing with, but it was obvious it had a lot of weight. I wondered how much Cisco knew.

"What's this?" asked Josalie, holding a brightly painted ceramic skull.

"Um, just some knickknack I picked up in Mexico. It's a Day of the Dead decoration."

"Oh, I thought it was some voodoo ingredient or something."

I gave her an odd look as she avoided eye contact. The teakettle whistled so I went to the kitchen. "You want one?"

"Sure."

"Milena?"

"Okay."

I smiled and set up three mugs, but by the time they were ready Milena was asleep. Josalie joined me at the kitchen island. We spoke in hushed voices.

"You weren't supposed to let them see you, Josalie."

"Whatever. They're cool." She took a sip and peeked at Milena dozing on the couch. "She's a party girl. You know she's a stripper?"

My first thought was that was just like Cisco. But I chewed my lip and gazed at Milena sleeping one off. Were we so different? I'd shown my naked body, not to the public but to Asmodeus, which was even worse in some ways. We all did what we needed to get by, no matter how hard or embarrassing. Living up to the moment, overcoming it—that was real strength.

It made me think I'd judged Milena too harshly. Pulling that shotgun on Ray in the Puzzle Box had taken grit. At the same time, she had that carefree attitude I'd always admired in Josalie. It was an attitude I could only experience vicariously. I appreciated it, needed it at times even, but it wasn't part of my DNA.

"They said some things," started Josalie in a measured tone.

Ah, the moment of truth. I canted my head, wondering what little tidbit my neighbor had learned about me. "I'm sure they did. They—"

"They said you can summon demons and your boss is an evil angel?"

I spit my tea all over the countertop. "Wha—?"

Her face flushed with excitement. "I know, crazy, right? I mean, Aaron's hiding a sweet bod, but an angel bod?"

"Don't call him that." My face soured. I was still frozen like a deer in headlights, but I wouldn't ever call Abaddon by his alias again. "He lied about who he was, about what he meant to me. Call him the Custodian now. That's all he gets."

She watched me, understanding my contempt because I'd bitched to her about him before, but not understanding enough to wipe the smirk off her face. "Are you just gonna ignore the demon summoning part?"

I swallowed. I hadn't been prepared to have the whole thing laid out to her this suddenly. "Like you said, it sounds crazy."

"Yeah, but it explains a few things. I've caught you talking to shadows before."

I fixed her with my most stern glare. "I do not talk to shadows."

"Uh-huh. Girl, you do some pretty strange things sometimes. So... are you like a witch or something? Can you do séances? Can you ask my dead *lola* what she did with my pet rabbit Fluffy when I was a kid?" Her eyes narrowed to slits. "One day he was gone and I just know the bitch did something."

I pinched the bridge of my nose. "I think that's more Cisco's realm."

"Really?"

"Oh, I get it. He spilled the beans about me but conveniently kept himself out of it, huh? Well, listen up. Cisco's a necromancer. He can talk to dead people and do all kinds of scary stuff."

Her jaw dropped in awe. "Get out!"

"I'm serious. Maybe he can even bring Fluffy back from the dead. You can have a little bunny skeleton hopping around."

"Gross. I wouldn't do that to Fluffy."

I blinked at her. This conversation had taken a weird turn, and we'd kind of buried the lede here. "So... You just take it in stride? I summon demons, end of story?"

"I mean, don't get me wrong, it's messed up. But Cisco said they're not really *demons* demons. And who am I to judge who you pray to?"

I shook my head with a smile. "I don't pray, Jo. It's not a religion."

"Whatever. I don't get it, but it's not like they're real. Not *really* real, like you or me or this counter or this mug."

"Or this statue," said Bernard indignantly.

"AH!!!"

Josalie dove away from the gargoyle and dropped her drink. The ceramic mug shattered and sent waves of tea across the polished cement. She awkwardly straddled the counter, screaming frantically, like there was a cockroach on the floor.

"It's gonna kill me, Shyla! Save yourself!"

I banished Bernard before Josalie had a heart attack. That was as close as I got to sympathy. Despite her wild eyes, I couldn't stop laughing. After a full minute of indulging myself, I helped Josalie to the floor. Her head was on a swivel, searching this way and that for the talking statue.

"Did you see that? Where'd it go? How many Kahlua Bombs did I have?"

I hugged her tight. She was trembling. "I'm sorry. That was mean of me. I just... You wanted to know."

She pulled away and studied the swirls of ash that disappeared before turning back to me. "You... You guys are serious..."

I hooked my fingers into my back pockets and shrugged.

"This is about as serious as it gets, Jo."

She drew a few long breaths, I cleaned up the mess, and I told my best friend who I really was.

Saved by the Bell

I didn't blame Josalie for needing a break after that. She'd gone through afternoon pancakes, light drinking, and a good scare. It was time to return to the humdrum of watching TV with her husband and waiting on the kids to get home. Say what you want about boring, but when the biggest decision of the day is where to get takeout for dinner, not a lot can go wrong.

I enjoyed some downtime in my bedroom until Cisco returned. I emerged but gave him space while he checked on Milena, who was passed out. Once his attention turned to me, I sat on the chair across from the couch.

"How'd you make out?" I asked.

He leaned into the cushion with a smile. "Better than expected. You?"

"Same." I recounted my creepy visit with John Conway and his animosity towards Helping Home. "Best of all, I found out what the pass token is."

"Let me guess. It's brass."

"Yes, actually." I wondered if the metal was significant for some spellwork he was familiar with.

"In the shape of a bell."

My eyebrows scrunched. "Okay, that's eerie. How'd you know that?"

"And it looks like this." He smugly pulled a pass token identical to mine from his pocket. "You see? Even when Cisco Suarez is assigned busy work, he comes through. Impressed yet?"

"Only that you always find a way to talk about yourself in the third person. But don't let it go to your head." I presented him with Conway's brass ornament.

His smugness evaporated. "That old man wants you to go in his stead."

"And they say you're just dumb muscle."

He drew his head back. "Who says that?"

I chuckled. "Is whoever you took that from gonna miss it?"

"That's the thing. I'm almost positive they'll need it back. I swiped it 'cause I figured you could forge a copy, but I guess that problem's solved for us."

"Sorry to rain on your parade, hotshot."

He snorted. "There's a lot more raining where that came from. I hate to admit it, but it was a smart play to watch the Helping Home office. Maybe there's something to your team of operators after all."

I shrugged off the compliment, more interested to hear what he'd discovered.

"So I was sitting on Helping Home's main office," he

rehashed, "seeing a whole lot of nothing and bored out of my mind, when a troupe of three visitors checked in."

"Recognize anybody?"

"I wasn't so lucky. Two women and one man, but they seemed a little... off. I couldn't place it. They were too stiff and didn't fit in with the rest of the rabble on the streets. So I got out of my jeep to get a look inside the office, and the next thing I know they're walking out the door. It was just a quick pickup." He flashed the brass bell, indicating the object of their visit.

"They'd arrived on foot," he continued, "so I followed after as they left. Two blocks to an indoor public storage facility. They used a small room in the back, and again turned on a dime and left. I went after them again. Only this time, when I turn the corner into an alley..."

I leaned forward in the chair.

Cisco rested back and brushed his hands with a cleaning motion. "They were gone."

Just as things were getting interesting. "Gone?"

"Gone."

"Where did they go?"

"They were gone. They vanished in broad daylight."

"Silvans?"

He lifted a finger. "I considered that. Silvans jumping back into the Nether, right? Thing is, the alley was paved with concrete. No space for a rabbit hole. And there weren't doors close by. No, I don't think these guys went down. I think they went up."

I pondered his conclusion for a full minute, running

down the possibilities. "You think they're jinns."

His eyes flashed recognition. "And they say you're just a pretty face."

"That comment still bothering you, huh?"

He shifted uncomfortably. "Anyway, besides the absence of rabbit holes, escaping to the Aether, or whatever you call it, makes sense. Jinns are essentially formless. They can't just vanish at any old time, like when they're in a building, but put them in open air and it's fair game."

"Thanks for the summoning lesson," I said with dry sarcasm.

"Oh, there's no summoning about it. They were clearly independent operators."

My skepticism showed plain. "You mean they can just enter and exit our world at will, no strings attached?"

"You've been hanging around hellions too much, Shyla. I'm surprised you don't know this." He shrugged. "But then, jinns never advertise what they are. You might remember a recent Caribbean drug kingpin I butted heads with. Connor Hatch was a jinn."

My sarcasm continued. "At this point I shouldn't be surprised at how experienced you are."

He grinned. "In more ways than one, Shyla. But stop hitting on me in front of my girlfriend."

Milena snored away in ignorance and I rolled my eyes hard.

"But their essence being fire and air comes with a practical drawback. They can't take anything physical along with them for the ride back home."

I nodded in understanding. "The High Elemental Plane is vaporous. It's not a physical space so much as a state of transcendence."

"I don't know about transcendence, but I know they can't spirit away a hunk of brass. So if they mean to attend a party using a key, they pick it up and keep it in storage until the day of the party, when they're back on our steppe."

I appreciated my academic knowledge of the plane being augmented by his practical facts. And the idea did make sense, except...

"What about Ray's summoning marker?" I asked. "He claimed the stone was carved from the very foundation of Mak... Ma... Somewhere in the High Elemental Plane."

Cisco blanched. "Was it Maqad?"

"Yes! You know it?"

"I don't just know it," he said with a grunt, "I've been there."

I took a moment to get over my shock. This time skepticism wasn't strong enough. "Impossible. You said it yourself. Nothing physical can travel there."

"Not impossible, given the right tools."

"No way. You might get me to believe a lot of things, but there's no way you went traipsing about the High. It's unheard of. There's nothing written about it in any texts. Except the Divine Comedy, maybe." I paused, wondering just where Dante's travels had led him.

He scoffed. "Summoners and their books. Believe what you want, Shyla, but I'm telling you like it is. There are five great satrapies in the Aether, and when it's time to choose a new ruler the satraps vote one of them to be king of kings. Maqad is the capital city of the shah, the seat of jinn power. Which explains this." He flipped his brass ornament around and presented the scripted name on the flat back. It read: Maqad.

I blinked. "Our silvan messenger wasn't inviting any old friend over to dinner. That summoning marker was a key to someone protected, someone who couldn't otherwise be summoned."

"Someone like an elemental on the royal staff."

Damn it all. That silvan had broken my circle to sever the link. It had left the elemental loose to go wherever it chose, but it had gone straight back to Maqad. The message was specifically for the shah.

"You said the silvan was royalty..." I realized aloud. "That means the charity banquet is about the king of the Low meeting the king of the High..."

The shadow charmer nodded darkly. "Crap, I should've seen it. Your boss is after a scepter, right?" He placed his hands in the air a couple of feet apart. "I bet it's about yea long, made of gold, and encrusted with jewels?"

"Gold fits the bill, but that's all we have. Why?"

"Because we've been thinking about this whole job wrong. The scepter's not just a valuable heirloom, it's a powerful artifact. It's the scepter of the shah. The Custodian's asking you to steal from the most powerful jinn in the world."

I wanted to deny it—we were making tons of leaps in logic—but the circumstantial evidence was overwhelming.

Besides, this was just like the Custodian.

"And I thought John Conway was the one with the hyperactive imagination," I muttered.

"What do you mean?"

"He hired me to destroy a summoning circle in the basement of the Conway House."

Cisco grinned. "You're doing a little moonlighting on the side. What's that make for you—three jobs at once?"

"You came to the best."

"So what's the rich guy worried about?"

"The usual. The end of the world. But when it comes to Abaddon, it might be a practical worry."

"You mean 'cause the guy is mentioned in *Revelation*?"

"Look at you, into books now." I smiled drily. "That's exactly why, but you have to understand. People like me learn to read between the lines of a lot of ancient texts. The most common interpretations aren't always the right ones."

He nodded along. "But?"

I checked the loft and scooted the chair closer. "But Abaddon's powerful. Like, *really* powerful. He stole the Ring of Solomon from a demon. It gives him untold power and allows him to operate unchecked on Earth." I paused, afraid to voice my concerns. "This job is another level for us. Granted, maybe it's my fault for peeking behind the curtain and discovering his true identity. Either way, Abaddon stealing a powerful relic from the shah of the High feels like an escalation."

"You think he's consolidating power." Cisco worked his jaw. "What do you think he wants to do with it?"

"I think I don't want to find out."

I mulled over the circumstances with a frown before retreating to the kitchen. This was more than a single-tea problem. I returned to my seat refreshed and determined.

"Okay, new plan. You and I are doing whatever it takes to keep this scepter out of Abaddon's hands."

He sniggered. "That's not gonna be easy. It's the whole reason for the heist. You think he's not gonna notice you not swiping the scepter?"

I shook my head firmly. "We need to set it up so we never have the chance. The score needs to backfire."

He leaned back with a whistle, mulling over the problem. "Maybe we can warn the shah," he suggested. "Get him out of Dodge before anything goes down."

I nodded at the possibility. "Whatever we do, we need to make sure it doesn't blow back on us. Abaddon won't take kindly to betrayal."

"You could blame me. I'm not scared of him."

"You should be. I wouldn't sic him on my worst enemy."

His eyes narrowed. "Thanks for that.... I think."

"Anyway, I vouched for you. Abaddon would take it out on me either way. What we need is something without a hint of our involvement." I considered the possibilities. "Even better than the shah leaving with the scepter early would be him never arriving at all. Or at least leaving it at home."

"Good luck with that," returned Cisco. "The jinn's cocky and powerful. He's unlikely to run from a threat, and a scepter like that is a symbol of his royal power. He's not leaving it behind."

"He might if he wants to protect it. But the real problem is getting a message to him beforehand. I don't have a summoning marker so I can't get him direct word. Summoning random elementals would leak the information for everyone to have, and going back to Ray's a risk since Abaddon already knows him."

"Yeah, that and he might try to kill us again."

I snorted. "It won't be easy sending a secret message to the shah. What about you? You've been to the High."

Cisco swallowed down a grimace. "I... kinda had help last time. Besides, it was one hell of a journey. I had to travel halfway across the world just to sneak into Maqad. And, I'm fuzzy on the shah's exact words, but he mentioned something about me never being welcome in the Aether ever again."

My eyelids fluttered in contempt. That's what happened when you set a bull loose in a china shop. So our practical options were exceedingly limited. What else was new?

Cisco fidgeted, seemingly uncomfortable with inaction. "Enough talk about angels, then. Isn't it about time we looked into the stiges?"

I cleared my throat. That was my end of our deal. "Of course, but let's do it tonight when Milena's awake. We want to look into helping her too." I hopped to my feet. "Besides, don't you think you need to get that pass token back to where you found it before anybody notices it missing?"

He frowned at the piece of brass, and then stood and slid

it into his back pocket. "Fair enough. It's a date." We headed to the door, but he lingered and held it open, turning to me. "But seriously, who says I'm just dumb muscle?"

I shoved him and his fragile ego outside.

Group Session

I stood on the balcony overlooking the pool. The platform ran the length of my loft and was one of only a few such units with the amenity. The night was cool but pervasive and heavy. Even though it hadn't rained all day, moisture clung to the air in an omnipresent fashion.

Bernard let Cisco and Milena in the front door. She'd woken up some time ago and figured a fancy dinner would do them good. I returned inside to the elevated steel platform that led to the balcony. It was only a few steps high but still a satisfying perch. I leaned on the railing and noted their somber mood.

Milena was sober, refreshed by activity and meal, but still ragged around the edges. Cisco was quiet. Neither engaged in their usual chipper banter. I guess everyone knew it was showtime.

"You guys ready?" I asked.

"Might as well get it over with," said Milena.

My boots clunked down the metal steps and toward the dining area. Bernard came in step at my side and I rubbed the top of his head.

"I hope the old witch is well," he remarked.

"No you don't," I chuckled.

Bernard erupted into a swirl of dissipating ashes. I tapped the table so the others would gather round on my way to the fridge. I poured milk into a small saucer and set it on the glass top.

"What's that?" asked Cisco. "A summoning tribute?"

"Of a sort."

I waved my hand and a small ball of fur sprang into existence atop the table. Milena flinched. Cisco put on a stoic display but his muscles were taut. They stared in fascination as pink fingers and toes reached out of the furball, steadying itself and revealing two gaping hazel eyes between a pink nose and rounded ears.

"*Que* cute!" cried Milena. "You look like a fat lemur!"

The hellion's eyes narrowed. "The name's Feifei, you succubus." The creature's nose sniffed the air, guiding it to the saucer. "Ah, the love of my life. Oat milk!" She buried her face and started slurping.

I arched an eyebrow. "Good to see you too, Feifei."

"Bah, we've seen each other before."

I crossed my arms and waited while she finished my offering. Feifei could be a handful, but I'd never seen her more docile than after a bowl of oat milk.

The little hellion sat back with a satisfied burp and wiped her mouth with knobbly fingers. "What's this one's problem?" she asked, pointing to Cisco. "He can't talk?"

"His problem is why you're here," I answered smoothly.

"He's had a run-in with some hellions recently and wanted to do a little research. Naturally, I thought of you."

"Naturally," she groaned. "Humans are always pulling Feifei into their troubles."

"This one doesn't require any field work. Just a chat." I flicked an iron coin with my thumb. She snatched it before it hit the table and shoved it into her fur.

"Fine," she said. "What do you wanna know?"

I turned to Cisco expectantly.

"What do you know about stiges?" he asked coarsely.

She barked in disgust. "Basque witches who hail from Stygia. They're flesh-eaters with powerful magic." She peered inquisitively at him. "More powerful than yours, I can tell you that."

"I wouldn't be so sure."

Feifei scoffed. "What a surprise. I've never seen a cocky human before. How old are you? Thirty, forty years? I was born before your modern calendar started. Spare Feifei your stige fairy tales."

If the admonishment had an effect on Cisco, he didn't show it. "I didn't read about the stiges in books," he said coolly. "I ran into one in the Nether. She escaped before I could choke the life out of her."

The hellion did something between gasping and snorting. Her eyes strained and she braced her hands on the table. At first I thought she was laughing, but she hacked and choked and arched her back painfully. Before I could ask if she was okay, she spat out a hairball the size of my fist. Everybody took a step away from the table.

"Look what you made me do!" she griped.

I grabbed a paper towel roll and balled it around my hand, once, twice, four times for good measure. I wiped the hairball and set it on the saucer before it had a chance to soak through the paper. I carried the mess to the kitchen and opened the garbage can. After a brief deliberation, I dropped everything, saucer and all, into the trash. I returned to the table with a spray bottle of bleach.

"You..." started Feifei, "saw a stige in the Elemental Planes?"

He nodded. "Why is that significant?"

"Shyla, you tramp, explain it to the ignoramus."

I smiled. It looked like I finally had knowledge Cisco didn't.

"It's something like this," I said. "You know the basics. Hellions can't freely enter the Material Plane. It's not just a matter of not being allowed, it's that they can't pull it off if they want to. Which is where people like me come in."

"I get it," he said. "Hellions need summoners. You think the silvans might have something to do with that."

"It's logical."

"I don't think these ladies follow logic."

"He's right," interrupted Feifei. "You can't summon stiges. Their spellwork is too strong. I'm not even sure a circle could hold them. But get to the good part. He asked about the Nether."

I was surprised by Feifei's conclusion but didn't outright deny it. When it came to her opinions, I learned long ago to keep an open mind. Ego was the worst thing a summoner could bring to an encounter with a demon.

"The Elemental Planes are raw and undefined," I explained. "They're the primordial edges of Creation. If there was some kind of doorway to Hell, a weakening of the walls so to speak, it would make sense to find it there."

"Okay," he said calmly, "but didn't you say it was against the rules? Isn't the entire point of Creation to keep the evil demons out?" He turned to Feifei. "No offense."

"Ha!" she laughed. "I like this one."

Great. Even Feifei was teaming up against me. Oat milk bought an audience but not loyalty, apparently.

"Angels keep hellions out," I agreed. "But remember my explanation of the creation of the Elemental Planes? The High was the intentional outcome and the Low was the byproduct. The end result is that no one polices the Low. Angels might visit, but if there's one place bulk demonic activity can go unnoticed, it's there."

Feifei smiled from ear to ear. "She's a little slow for a student, but she gets to the point."

Cisco turned to Milena, who was a little wobbly on her legs. "So we were right to follow the silvans. They know more than they're letting on."

She nodded and took a seat at the table. Feifei watched her curiously.

"How do we fight them?" asked Cisco.

The hellions eyes widened. "Fight them? No, no, you don't fight stiges."

He huffed. "They have to have a weakness."

"Sure they do. Angels. The last time a stige lost a fight

was when they were collectively cast down before the Flood. And don't think for a second you had the upper hand on one of those witches. You saw what she wanted you to see. If you ask me, the whole thing was nothing but a test or a distraction."

He ground his teeth at the suggestion that his victory had been a ruse. "Listen up, you little munchkin..."

"How about we change the subject?" I cut in. "Remember, we're here for Milena. Feifei, the stiges did something to her, poisoned her with their blood."

The critter's eyes widened. "And you lived to tell the tale? Impressive." The obese guinea pig scooted across the table and held out her hands. "May I?"

Milena lifted her head and traded glances between Cisco and Feifei. She looked into the old lady's bulbous green-and-brown eyes and offered her hand in return. Feifei flipped it over and ran tiny fingers across her palm.

"Ah," she muttered, "you speak the truth. There is some of the World Below in you, though you are no demon yourself. I was wrong to call you a succubus, though perhaps not far off."

"I'm not human anymore," she groaned.

"In a technical sense, no, but why harp over semantics, child? You are... changing... growing. At least if that is the path you choose."

"And if I don't choose?" she piped. Cisco hands went to Milena's shoulders reassuringly.

Feifei sighed. "Change is a fulcrum, child. You may choose to melt in this fire or be forged into something greater. Your resolve will determine the hammer's blows."

Milena's lips curled at the simple wisdom.

With nothing more to add, Feifei's eyes snapped to Cisco and she reached out to him. The shadow charmer stepped past Milena and offered his hand.

"Hmm," murmured Feifei, eyes flaring slightly. "You have something inside you I find familiar, like my world, but different. It's Earthly. A powerful beastly presence."

He swallowed. "Opiyel."

"Is that an angel?" I asked.

He shook his head once. "An Arawak god. The Shadow Dog."

"Yes, Shyla," said Feifei. "Gods can be many things. Hellions, angels, even spirits. But this one has something more. I see leathery black wings..."

"The Wings of Night," he revealed, amused at her proficiency in palm reading.

"If you say so. They act to protect you and guide you, but they also serve as a bridge builder. They're a path between worlds."

I couldn't read Cisco's expression as he processed the news. Maybe it was new information to him, maybe it wasn't, but he didn't volunteer anything else.

I grumbled inwardly. Feifei was the perfect combination of wise and knowledgeable. Unfortunately, when it came to looking inside me, she had nothing to say about the Dark One. I sometimes suspected it had to do with prior commitments. They were a common obstacle for hellions. Asmodeus, for example, could never tell me the truth about

Abaddon because the angel had gotten to him first.

I grew frustrated, by my inability to help myself but also offering my friends nothing more than a parlor show. Palm reading wasn't why we were here. We'd gleaned little about the stiges. I would need to dig deeper into my grimoire.

And then it came to me. Something that might have been a coincidence but was more likely to be connected in some unseen way. I blurted out my train of thought.

"Balam's dead, right?"

Everyone turned to me, and Feifei's eyes narrowed. "It's not healthy to speak ill of kings."

"Even dead ones?"

"*Especially* dead ones, Shyla."

"It's just a question. Balam was the archon of Stygia, was he not? I had a hellion tell me he was deposed not too long ago. Maybe the stige activity has to do with the new archon."

Feifei's eyes blinked, one and then the other, as she brought my question into focus. "It is possible," admitted the crone, "but, as with everything in Hell, it is difficult to ascertain. A new archon hasn't been announced for hundreds of years."

"But this can't be a coincidence. We're talking about Stygia here."

"And they're not the only ring experiencing tremors. There's Kur, of course."

My brow furrowed. "What about Kur?"

"Didn't that brutish gargoyle of yours tell you about his home?"

"Politics isn't Bernard's strong suit."

"Big surprise." She shrugged. "I suppose it started before you were born, so it isn't news. Astaroth has been stepping up caretaker duties."

"But Inanna's still the archon." If memory served, she was an ancient Mesopotamian goddess of harlots. She'd ruled Kur for thousands of years ever since wresting it from her sister Ereshkigal. As far as goddesses go, she's as old as they come, having gone through various permutations as Ishtar, Astoreth, and Aphrodite. "Wait a minute... You're saying Inanna's missing too?"

"I said nothing of the sort!" snapped the furball. "I do not speak ill of the archons. I only mention that they rule at their pleasure, and it is not for us to examine such things."

She watched me in warning, afraid of saying anything else that might draw the wrath of the kings and queens of the World Below.

"You've gotten your coin's worth," she spat, "and then some. Leave these things in the pages of Estever's book, but speak them aloud to me no more."

Feifei curled up tightly and winked out of existence. Cisco made a move to catch her, but he was too slow. He would've been unable to physically hold her in this space anyway, as I hadn't compelled Feifei with hexagrams and circles. He cursed and stomped away. I tried to meet Milena's eyes, but she stared at the now-empty table.

I took a breath and followed Cisco to the other side of the room. "Sorry I couldn't get more," I said softly. "There might be other options. Or, if you wanted to bail now, I'd understand."

His eyes locked on mine.

"You know," I explained, not dishonestly, "you could take Milena back to Miami. I'll tell the Custodian we don't need you anymore." I took a long breath. "It'll be safer considering how the heist has to go down."

He stared at me, probably wondering if he should take me up on my offer. He had Milena to think about, after all, and the poor girl didn't seem too thrilled at her prognosis.

"I can't believe you're serious," he finally said. "I'm not about to leave you high and dry here. Especially since we can get more answers at the Conway House."

"That's a long shot."

"The longer, the better."

I hissed. "I'm just saying, if I were in your shoes, I'd re-evaluate the play here. Going through with the score is looking less and less profitable."

"That's not the point." He glanced at Milena and worked his jaw. "I'm not here for profit, Shyla. That's your game. Maybe you'd see that if everything wasn't business to you. Let's go, Milena. We'll get out of here tonight, sleep in a hotel close by."

They collected their things and hurried to the door. I almost said something to stop them, but I was angry at the guilt Cisco's words had brought on. They stepped outside and Cisco turned to study me a moment.

"Look, I said I would help you and I will. You and me are doing this thing. There's no stopping it so don't even try."

Boots on the Ground

The next day was filled with various prep work. Jobs like this involved a lot of moving parts. As the Handler, I was thankful to skirt the paperwork. Identities, bank accounts, and associations were invaluable, but they sure were boring.

With as much as we'd already accomplished, today was a matter of crossing the "t"s and dotting the "i"s. I dropped the brass bell ornament off to a not-so-reputable jeweler I worked with. I paid him extra for a rush job. He would sand down the engraving and replace it with a new cover name in the same script.

I juggled my phones with various coordination efforts. The Wire had come through with his Lock-E contact. There were to be twenty-two security personnel on site. It was a big number considering it didn't include whatever enforcers the supernatural donors brought with them. Then there was the fact Lock-E would be implementing radio interference. The Wire was still working on a way for us to remain in live communication during the score, but it wasn't a sure thing.

I had little contact with the Custodian and the Lead. Believe me, I welcomed it. The thought of going against Abaddon made me nervous. I kept thinking up angles and none of them played out in ways that kept me breathing. As much as I hated to admit it, I had to play the good little operator for a while, and that meant revealing the shah and his scepter to the Custodian.

Besides, for all I knew he already had the same info. With an angel lording over me, anything could be a test of faith.

I did another drive-by of the Conway House, this time wearing a red wig and driving a rental car. I circled the block and compared my vantage with satellite views, but the property and surrounding area enjoyed the natural camouflage of a lush tree canopy. For some reason, the few images I did find with decent angles were lower resolution than usual. I wondered if there was some advanced magic protecting the place, but it seemed far-fetched.

Yeah, silvans meeting jinns in a secret basement with a divinity gate, and protection magic was far-fetched. I needed to constantly remind myself that I was in the big leagues now. That and assure myself I wasn't in over my head.

I heard less from Cisco than I'd expected, but then I had given him the day off. His relationship with Milena was strained in light of the little help I could offer. To be honest, I felt personally responsible. Which was stupid, of course.

Hellions were savvy, capable creatures. If the stiges had

done something to Milena, there likely was nothing I could do about it. I needed to stop putting the weight of the world on my shoulders. It wasn't how I'd survived this far, and it wouldn't be how I ultimately got out from under this.

I stuffed the guilt deep down and drove on. Casing the property was still a no-go. With Conway's information, it wasn't even necessary. I didn't see anything that concerned me except for Lock-E, and they were the ones that were gonna let us through the front gate.

I had to admit, that boring paperwork stuff had its uses.

I picked up a vanilla latte on the way home, and then showered and griped to Bernard about things. You know, the usual. As had become a ritual of late, I pulled out my grandmother's grimoire and browsed the appendix of demons. Just a little light reading for a summoner.

I had never heard of anything like the stiges. After confirming there was no overlap with other known hellions, I added an entry for them and transcribed what little information we had so far. Witches with black owl consorts.

"Hey Bernard," I said offhandedly, lying with my stomach on the bed and my socks in the air, "how come you never told me Inanna was missing?"

He poked his head up from the floor. "Since when have you been interested in Kur politics?"

I shrugged. "Remember I was burned by not knowing Balam was deposed? I lose my power over hellions when I'm not aware which archons are active."

"And what makes you think the Queen of the Night isn't active?" His face sagged. "You've been talking to that little crone. I thought she didn't partake in gossip."

"She didn't say much, just that Astaroth has been ruling in her stead."

"Sure, for fifty years or so, but that's a drop in the bucket."

"Don't you think it's weird you haven't seen her for fifty years?"

"I haven't seen her for two hundred and fifty years, and not particularly. The kings and queens of Hell don't invite the general populace over for cakes and tea."

I snorted and almost coughed up my latte. "Fair enough."

"If it makes you feel better, I haven't seen Astaroth the last fifty years either, and he's the one supposedly holding down the fort. You know I care little for such things, especially with being up here so much."

I nodded begrudgingly. It wasn't like I was shaking hands with the president of the United States on a daily basis either. It just seemed a waste having a familiar from Kur and not knowing useful details.

"Tell me about Inanna," I requested. "What kind of ruler is she?"

The gargoyle's eyes seemed to glow in the darkening twilight, so it was very obvious when they narrowed. "Shyla, I hope you'll excuse me for speaking lightly. The rings of Hell aren't known for their freedoms. Simple speech can often offend."

"Right. No Bill of Rights in Hell." I flipped the grimoire to the section describing the various archons. "Just give me your general impressions."

He sat up straight and recited. "Inanna is the Queen of Heaven turned the Queen of Night, the Morning Star turned to Evening. She is the eight-pointed Star of Venus, the Patron of Uruk, worshipped by the Sumerians, Akkadians, Babylonians, and Assyrians. She has many names and is a goddess of war and justice, sex and love."

"I have the Cliff Notes in front of me," I said drily. "I'm asking what type of ruler she is. She stole Kur from her sister Ereshkigal, right? Tell me about that."

He grumbled. "There was a time, perhaps, when the Queen of the Night didn't get her due. She was young and impetuous, her decisions rash and impulsive. But no one could ever say she wasn't formidable. Inanna has always increased her station in life the old way, by being stronger and more cunning than those she takes from. Even when it's her sister."

I pressed my lips out, trying to get a feel for the convoluted mythology of gods and their families. It was the Mesopotamian religions that had inspired the dysfunctional relationships of the more famous Greek Pantheon. Hell, one of Inanna's presentations *was* Aphrodite, so inspiration wasn't a literal-enough term.

"And do you think it's possible her conniving caught up to her?" I asked. "Maybe someone finally outmaneuvered the Queen of the Night?"

Bernard held back a laugh with a smirk. "Deposed by her son? It would never happen. Astaroth is the biggest mama's boy you've ever seen. And I can say that loudly because it would make both him and his queen proud."

I chuckled. It was a curious impression of a powerful duke of Hell. Astaroth, unlike his mother, was well-known in demonology circles, but that hardly reduced Inanna's allure. She was almighty and old-school, more so than many medieval grimoires touched upon. And if she wasn't as popular today, so what? I was intimately familiar with the idea of the power behind the power.

That led me to ponder other rivalries in Hell. There was Jackal, of Dis, and his allegiance to Paimon and Lucifer. Jackal was a hellion I hoped never to encounter again, though I couldn't deny that meeting him had been fortuitous. He was the one who'd revealed my lineage. I was a descendant of King Solomon, probably the most famous summoner in history. It helped explain my affinity with demons, my wielding of the Sigillum Dei, and possibly why Bernard had taken a shine to me. My royal lineage had otherwise been a burden to me, it being the prime reason my father was abducted to Hell and why I was in the service of an angel who now possessed the Ring of Solomon.

I shut the grimoire and tried to clear my head for a few hours with some classic rock. All things considered, it turned into a nice evening. It's impossible to listen to Cream's *Dance the Night Away* without losing yourself for a moment. Soon enough, I was like a normal woman kicking around the house with her dog, if that dog was a three-hundred-pound half-immortal gargoyle.

At the stroke of midnight, I opened the wardrobe in my bedroom and revealed the mirror within. The image of a lean man with ashy hair and a dark goatee coalesced. To the other operators on the team, he was known as Bedrock, but I knew the demon's true name.

"Up and at them, Asmodeus."

Mirror, Mirror

The demon groaned and arched his back in a long stretch. "Ah yes, time for your brief reunion with the unfortunate Paulson Crowe."

"Actually, my father can wait. We should talk, you and I."

Asmodeus moved in a slithering fashion, like a snake. His serpentine tail only added to the aesthetic. "I wasn't aware you had any further interest in our chats."

"Don't get your hopes up. I just want to know what you know about this convocation business."

He yawned. "Oh, don't bore me with such banalities, Shyla. You used to be more exciting than this."

"Your dreams of pleasure between us are long gone. We talk on my terms because I'm the only one who knows of your betrayal. One word to Abaddon and..."

His already pale face blanched. "No need to remind me, dearest. I understand the position you have me in. It would serve to remember that my betrayal was in assistance to

142

you."

"And you only helped me to help yourself."

He splayed his hands to the side as if to say it was settled. "There, you see? We are both being trod upon. It's clear who our mutual enemy is."

I inwardly recoiled at the thought of Asmodeus and I on the same team. I was indeed aware of his precarious position. He wanted out from under Abaddon's thumb just as I did. The thing was, he couldn't outright assist me in betraying the angel. He was bound by the Ring of Solomon and his word.

The demon had helped me in the past by arranging things so I'd learn the information I needed, but he couldn't directly tell me anything. Our interactions were plain and unrevealing on the surface, but behind the scenes they kicked off a series of events like a Rube Goldberg device, a bunch of disparate and precarious elements come together with an impossible result. I was hoping for a similar shot in the dark.

"Tell me about the convocation."

Asmodeus rolled his eyes. "A boring meeting full of stuffy bores. Convocations exist solely so self-important people can blather about self-important things, all in service to feeling more self-important than all the other self-important people in attendance. I already dread having to bear it."

I narrowed my eyes. "Wait, you're attending?"

"Were you not told?" His lips sharpened into a devilish grin. "I'm the head of the team, Shyla. On paper, anyway.

Bedrock must assist his operators. I have a vested interest in the heist going off without a hitch. I'll be there in person."

"How?"

"Fix your piercing eyes on another target. How I attend is not your worry."

"It is if I say it is."

He shook his head and brought an edge to his voice. "You have only one goal. Get the staff and get out."

Asmodeus didn't like being micromanaged. It was bad enough he had an angel compelling him, but to be subservient to a human was the ultimate shame. He was quicker to anger these days. And more prone to making mistakes.

"I thought we were looking for a scepter," I said.

His brow relaxed and he gave an easygoing shrug. "Staff, scepter, rod. Tomato, tomahto, marinara. Worry less about form and more about function."

I lightly worked my jaw. "The scepter's powers. I'm concerned about them too."

He scoffed. "Who said the scepter has power? Certainly not me. *That* would be against the terms of our benefactor."

There. That was definitely an insinuation. A divergence of service and desire. He as much as confirmed Cisco's hunch that the scepter was powerful.

"Why does Abaddon want it?" I asked.

"That question is reserved for the man himself, so to speak. He wishes to own it, but there's a great difference between a rightful owner and a righteous owner."

My eyes flashed. "You realize we're all thieves, right?"

"Perhaps, but not all hands are hallowed."

I never liked demonic wordplay. I could never tell if they were providing helpful riddles or delighting in toying with prey. Maybe to spite him, I moved the crosshairs back to him.

"What role will you be serving at the convocation?"

"I told you, Shyla—"

"I need to know what everyone on the team is doing."

He chuckled. "Maybe you're just getting tickled at the thought of having me around?"

I didn't give him the satisfaction of a response. "Why are you attending, Asmodeus?"

He snorted. "Assisting the theft, of course. I'll be a distraction. Don't concern yourself with me, lest you be distracted too. I think it's about time our chat was done."

"Wait."

Surprisingly, he paused. Perhaps it was because he was obligated to let me speak with my father. It was my most important term, and demons understood terms.

But in this case, there was something else I was hoping to hear about. It was a risk mentioning it, since he could pass my words on to Abaddon, but I figured it safe enough.

"What do you know of the stiges?" I asked in a measured tone.

Asmodeus watched me with a blank face for long enough that it was a reaction itself.

"My, my," he said softly, "but then you *are* clever. Cleverer than you let on." He almost smiled. "You were one step ahead of me with my unmasking. And now you're investigating the witches of Stygia. This is the work of that Jackal, isn't it?"

"No," I said plainly. "I don't expect to ever see him again."

He watched me a moment and nodded, choosing to believe me. "Then tell me, Shyla, which demon *is* whispering in your ear?"

It had only been Cisco, but the statement unnerved me. It insinuated that I couldn't trust the shadow charmer. That maybe he had ulterior motives. I refused to believe that. Guys like him, they wore their hearts on their sleeves.

"Where do the stiges fit into this?" I demanded.

His eyebrows shot up. "With the convocation? They don't. But they're ambitious cunts, I can tell you that much. I wouldn't turn my back on them, and I was a king of Hell." He huffed in annoyance. "Now I'm afraid I have a previous engagement, and our time is up. Shall you be speaking to dear old dad tonight?"

I swallowed my anger. Asmodeus hadn't helped me, but he'd accommodated me enough to fulfill his bargain. It was just like a demon to follow the fine print.

"Dad," I muttered.

I shook away the worry and put on a smile for the person who'd gotten us buried in this sordid business to begin with.

Coffee and Breakfast

I was in bed when the smell of fresh bread and coffee hit me. The initial wave of pleasantry evaporated as I realized I was awake and someone was in my loft. I jerked up, bedsheet held to my neck, and peered through the bookcase divider that walled off my bedroom. With a healthy lean I could make out Cisco in the kitchen.

My eyes fell to the gargoyle standing watch at the edge of the bedroom. Bernard had let him in.

"You're supposed to wake me," I whispered, slipping out of bed and moving behind the changing screen.

"We felt you could use the rest," he returned indignantly. "Today's the big day, and your sleep was restless last night."

I threw on the first shirt I found, which happened to be a Led Zeppelin tie-dye, and then balanced the good vibes with my black leather pants. This early, I'd usually opt for something more comfortable, but Cisco was a work friend so I needed my game face on. I stormed out of the room, slipping my arms through my jacket.

I was about to chew him out, but the closer I got to the kitchen, the better whatever he was cooking smelled.

"I took the liberty of buying a few things," he commented with his back to me. "You need to try authentic Cuban coffee." He lifted one of those Italian stainless steel coffee pots from the stove and poured into a shot glass that had never seen anything but tequila. He turned to me for the first time and handed it over.

It was the smallest serving of coffee I'd ever seen, but one sip and my mood immediately brightened. The roast was dark and bitter but evened out with a *lot* of sugar. There was so much sugar the black coffee had a layer of tan cream on top. I swallowed the rest in another gulp.

Cisco grinned. "Good, right? I also picked up some real milk while I was at it."

"Oat milk is real milk."

"No, it's an abomination, and that's coming from a guy who brings roadkill back from the dead. You wanna eat?"

Only a necromancer could mention roadkill in one breath and breakfast in the next. He scooped scrambled eggs onto a plate and lathered butter on bread sliced from a long loaf. "This is Cuban bread. It's made with lard." He set it on the island. As I tasted the eggs, he poured a pot of warmed milk into a mug and dropped another shot of coffee into it.

"*Cafe con leche*," he relayed with a wink. "Good for what ails you." Then he lifted his own mug and relaxed against the edge of the stove.

I was so dumbstruck by the hospitality that I jammed

another forkful of eggs into my mouth to stall. Then I tried the toasted bread and capped it off with a sip of the Cuban version of a cappuccino.

"Let me show you," he said. "You dunk it, like this." Cisco dipped the tip of his toast into his coffee mug. When he drew it out, the crunchy buttery bread was soaked with brown. He bit off the whole end.

I blinked. I had some strange breakfast habits, but I wasn't gonna do *that*. I threw a hand up.

"What is going on here? Why are you in my house?"

He arched an eyebrow. "You didn't check your messages?"

I had. I checked my phones again. Neither had waiting texts.

Cisco chuckled and handed me his phone. It was open on a text message from a number I recognized. The Custodian had called for an early meeting. At my place, of course.

Cisco took his phone back. "I figured he was the type of guy to show up unannounced again. It's a bit you guys are doing, am I right?"

I rolled my eyes and hurried to my room to snap on my riding boots. The Custodian was messing with me for the sole purpose of showing me who was boss. Blindsiding me while I was asleep and nearly naked might take me down a notch. Cisco was being a bro by showing up early. Once I was ready to roll, I hurried back to my breakfast.

"I do have to say," started Cisco, "I don't like that the guy has my phone number. I've only had this burner for a few weeks. You give it to him?"

"Of course not. We've been using my private line, but you were calling my business phone in the weeks before. It's in Bedrock's name. The Custodian probably pulled the records."

Just another show of control from my boss. And he was reaching out to Cisco now.

We finished breakfast while I updated him on the latest developments. It wasn't long before the Custodian's measured knock rapped my door. He was ten minutes early to his own meeting, which meant he'd wanted to surprise me alone.

I opened in full leathers and greeted him with my falsest morning-person impression. His gray eyes tracked me like a predator before darting to Bernard and Cisco. "Early start, I see." He sounded disappointed.

"I'm eager to get a move on," I answered, oblivious to his sentiment.

"You should've said jinns were involved," said Cisco, lasering right to the point, as usual.

"Jinns..." intoned the Custodian, slowly and intentionally, as if testing the word.

Cisco scoffed. "Don't tell me you didn't know we were stealing the scepter from the shah of Maqad?"

The Custodian's eyes flared. "Interesting."

"Come on," I pressed. "Cut the shit with us. We need to know these details."

But the angel was honestly taking it in. After a moment of contemplation, he adjusted his wire glasses and explained. "I heard through a source, one even Bedrock doesn't have access to..."

He eyed me in warning. His source was probably angelic, and he still believed Cisco didn't know his true identity.

"The scepter would make an appearance at a convocation," he continued. "I didn't know the where, the when, or the who. The silvan messenger filled in the first two, and your discovery just filled in the last. Excellent work."

Cisco and I traded a look. He seemed to accept the answer, though I was skeptical. People in our line of work guarded secrets closely. It was why I'd left out mention of the divinity gate in my reports. It didn't pertain to the job, it could earn me a little extra money on the side, and it was always possible I could use the information to my advantage. When you're up against an angel, you need any weapon you can find.

"You know, Cisco," he added, "if you continue to impress like this, there may be a permanent place for you on this team."

Something stirred in me. Envy of the Custodian directing his praise toward someone else... Anger that he assumed it was Cisco who'd discovered the jinn connection. He had, of course, but the automatic assumption rankled me. I was the summoner, wasn't I?

Then again, I'd never seen a jinn before. My experience with the High Elemental Plane was mostly relegated to actual elementals. And then, with my affinity to the World Below, it had been hellions who'd become my stock in trade. My understanding of jinnkind came from the same bunch of musty books I constantly warned people about believing whole cloth.

"Don't count on it," said Cisco in answer. "I'm still learning to be a team player."

"And the scepter?" I cut in. "What does it do?"

The Custodian hiked a shoulder a little too casually. "It's just a symbol of power. It makes perfect sense for a ruler from a rich tradition to possess it. At least until we take it from him."

It was clear he wasn't telling everything, but what else was new? His offhand comments only made me want the scepter more. But if I was going to risk the angel's wrath by failing to steal it, I had to make sure it was worth it. That meant figuring out what the damn thing was first.

Further talk was stilted until the rest of our team showed up. The Wire carried an info dump in a briefcase, everything we'd need to know about the charity banquet's security measures. The Lead's blonde hair was permed straight, with dark highlights, and she wore expensive long lashes. She wasn't even in costume yet and she looked the part of a pampered daughter and premier socialite. Knowing her, she could answer every question about her cover half asleep.

We got down to business immediately, and it wasn't long before we had to address the elephant in the room. The Wire and the Lead were average joes, so to speak. They knew about silvans and hellions, but only as far as they needed to in pursuit of the job.

This job was extra special, and it was time to brief them

on a new type of supernatural creature.

"Jinns are like demons in some ways," I told the team. "Nearly indistinguishable on the surface. Much of Arabian myth blurs the line between the two types of beings."

That much was true, but there was a marked difference.

Jinns were free beings who enjoyed a special status in the lofty heights of Creation. Back in the day, they were duty-bound servants to the angels and, at times, even man. It wasn't lost on me that both demons and jinns purportedly helped build the Temple of Solomon.

"Jinns are primal beings," I explained, "but they're not elementals. You can't summon them or command them."

I paused at the thought and locked eyes with the Custodian. Popular culture is rife with stories of genies being commanded or controlled. The Ring of Solomon was a particularly interesting case. It made me wonder what the trouble of the heist was for, but I didn't voice my question in front of the group.

"They're very powerful," I added. "Which means the last thing we want out of them is a fight." I looked to the Custodian, to make sure he agreed with my point.

"Correct," he said. "And with this group, it shouldn't need to be said, but never, ever make a deal with a jinn." Wide eyes met the instruction.

"It's for your protection," said Cisco. "Celestial law. Jinns can't hurt humans unless they enter a willing contract together. Keep from doing that, and they're no more harmful than the air they're made of."

The Custodian regarded the shadow charmer with

something like newfound respect. Cisco's words weren't adorned with the fluff of fanciful tales or academic jargon. He spoke with the no-nonsense surety of experience.

"That said," he conceded, "there'll be plenty of people at the banquet that can and will gladly harm you, humans included. Which is why I'm with the Handler. The last thing we want is a fight."

After some time, the team broke into groups to talk over specifics. I brought the Custodian aside, eager to glean any additional info before we set out for the Conway House.

"What about your ring?" I whispered, very careful that no one could overhear. The mention alone made his face tense, indicating the thin ice I was treading on. "It's said to have commanded jinns. It was what built the First Temple. Why can't you just use it to ask for the scepter and call this heist done?"

His lips pressed together tightly. "Another time and place for that answer. And don't you dare mention it again. As far as you're concerned, this ring doesn't exist." The Custodian looked deeply into my eyes as something orange behind his flared. "This is your score, Shyla, and I hope, for your sake, that everything goes exactly as planned."

The House in the Hills

It was almost eight o'clock, and the evening was so beautiful I would've framed it in a picture if I could. The moon was high and full, the breeze flowing through the hills, crisp. It was the perfect setting for a midnight stroll with a side of cat burglary.

Aside from recognizing niceties, my actual travel accommodations left a little to be desired. The Custodian had acquired a pricey elongated Cadillac XTS limousine. The chrome paneling impressed ever so slightly while the glossy black blended with all the other professional cars. The Wire wore a simple business suit and posed as our driver while the Custodian and the Lead were dressed to the nines in the cabin.

Cisco and I? We were tucked on the floor beneath a beverage table. The original plan had involved a more elaborate false seat and me contorting in ways my body hadn't attempted in twenty years. Thankfully Cisco's shadow magic provided that extra layer of security. The two of us merely had to lie out of sight and he assured we'd be fine.

A line of cars backed up on the street outside the Conway House. The iron gate was wide open. I didn't dare peek, but our intel said there'd be a team of four Lock-E personnel at the entry. That was in addition to the greeters and helper staff directing the drivers. It was smart of the security team to leave the busy work for other staff. It meant they were one hundred percent focused on their jobs, which was one hundred percent about looking for people like me.

As our car reached the head of the line, the Wire buzzed down his window. He offered his credentials and answered a few questions. I heard mention of the pass key but the Lead had it in her purse and didn't need to show it yet. The staff member directed the car inside.

And just like that, we cleared the first hurdle. We were past the front gate.

The property was a compound more than a residence, with various stages of entry. The exterior gate was only the beginning. The private roadway curved between thick Mediterranean brush as it ascended the slope.

"There's a parking level here," announced the Wire. "I can't believe how big it is. It's like we're visiting a museum. They're directing me up to the house."

The car winded higher up the road until it wheeled around a large driveway. From the floor of the car, I could see the tall central fountain as we rounded it and came to a stop.

Cisco put his hand on my shoulder. "Don't be scared,"

he whispered.

The back door opened. I was immediately drawn backward, like I was falling through the floor, yet I hadn't moved an inch. I felt both present and disconnected at the same time, an intimate out-of-body experience.

A valet holding the door open smiled. "Good evening, sir and madam. Names please."

The Lead stuck a sharp heel outside and offered her gloved hand. "Diana Halpert and my guest."

The man respectfully helped her from the car. She wore a dashing red dress that hugged her thin waist. Long slits down each side revealed legs a short girl like me would've killed for. The Lead had the lithe build of a model who could command the room with a walk.

The valet peeked into the car as the Custodian exited. I could've sworn he looked right at me. Either way, he showed no reaction. "And the token, madam?"

She unsnapped her clutch and flashed it.

"Excellent," conveyed the valet. "They'll take it at the table. Your driver can wait in the lot or return to the property later."

The Custodian silently took position behind the Lead. If he looked nervous, it had nothing to do with the heist. I was coming to think he despised the banality of everyday social interactions. His outfit was simpler, a casual jacket over a thin sweater. The idea was to play second fiddle to the Lead's starring role.

"I'll keep him close at hand," assured the Lead, loud enough so the Wire could hear.

"Excellent. Then you may proceed to the greeters on the right side of the house. Do not attempt to enter the front door. The banquet is in the back."

They nodded thanks but the valet was already jotting down the limo's plate number on a green ticket. He ripped a stub away and waited as the Wire lowered his window.

"Keep this ticket on the dashboard please. We'll collect it upon your departure."

We'd already been briefed on the security precautions. The brass bells were being taken by the greeters. This prevented hijinks with ins-and-outs involving passing the key to another party. It also let Helping Home track who was in the party and who wasn't.

This was a complication, because if we stole the scepter and disappeared, ours might be the only pass token left unclaimed. Fake name or no, that would give the security team a lead that could point our way.

The parking ticket needing to be returned was a similar measure. If everything went according to plan, our exit would be just as legitimate as our entrance, and we wouldn't leave anything behind to remember us by. The Lead would be one among hundreds of guests. It was herd immunity in action.

"Should we slip out now?" asked Cisco after the window closed.

"No," said the Wire. "The parking platform looked perfect. It wasn't too crowded and lacks a dedicated security team."

Now that we were released from the grip of his shadow

magic, I took a calming breath. "Stick to the plan, Cisco."

"There was a plan?" he quipped.

I arched my eyebrow. He was playing it off like a joke, but I wondered how much he was kidding. He was the type of guy to react to things in the moment. The Custodian was right; I would need to babysit our necromancer.

The Cadillac pulled onto the parking level. "Damn, roving security," warned the Wire. "Stay put."

We waited while he found a nice corner to park in. He left the car running but exited and shut the door, and then he leaned against the back window so we could watch him. The Wire lit a cigarette at his lips and let out a relaxed breath of smoke. Besides returning a wave from another distant driver, nobody harassed him. A few minutes later, he put out his smoke and returned to his seat.

"Okay, the rover moved on. They're not too concerned about the drivers."

I emerged from under the table with a kink in my shoulder. I arched my back a few ways to work it out. The Wire unfolded a laptop and went to work. He hooked into their system through a Wi-Fi vulnerability.

"Can you tap into their security?" I asked.

"Piece of cake."

Cisco's eyes widened. "This is wild. It feels like *Mission: Impossible* or something."

"Try *Ocean's Eleven*," he corrected. "I'm not saving the world, just my bank account."

I was already scoping the perimeter through the black-tinted windows. Without the cabin lights on, no one could see inside. "This looks better than the satellite image let on," I said. "The brush has grown thicker. We can jump right in and climb to the house, away from the road."

Climb wasn't strictly accurate. While I wouldn't want to navigate the slope of wood mulch in heels, the hillside wasn't prohibitively steep. Cisco and I slipped out of the door flush with the edge of the parking lot and jumped into the bushes. Large, fan-shaped desert brush in various browns and greens camouflaged us.

With my jacket zipped up I wore all black. Cisco was still in blue jeans, but I'd convinced him to wear a black tee instead of the bright white tank top that would stand out in the moonlight. The shirt had been left behind by an old boyfriend and the AC/DC logo was mostly faded. It was about as professional as I could convince Cisco to be.

And don't get me started on the red cowboy boots. I begged and pleaded with him to change those, but he wouldn't budge. Ego trumps practicality every time.

The ground leveled out at the top of the hill, and we crouched at the edge of the brush. The pictures had done a poor job of conveying the scale of the place. The wide roundabout was almost as large as the parking lot below. The fountain was impressive, and the Conway House was a Frank Lloyd Wright masterpiece. Modern sensibilities were seamlessly fused with traditional design. The house seemed to grow out of the hill more than having been built atop it, and the walk-up porch and side walkways were built on different levels to accommodate the natural terrain. It was a striking facade.

The security was just as impressive. Another four-man crew watched the front, two at the door and two at the greeting table to the right of the house. We watched as a guest handed over their pass token and was waved by. They'd walk alongside the house and emerge in the backyard where the banquet was taking place.

While we never uncovered details on the so-called platinum members, what I was seeing lined up with our best-guesses. The front door wasn't for admission. Entry to the house would happen in the back, allowing travel to and from the banquet as necessary. The large veranda and lounge just inside all faced the backyard stage.

My phone buzzed. With security blocking short-range radio frequencies, we had to work around our usual methods. The team had a set of dummy cell phones that couldn't be traced, all logged into an encrypted chat over guest Wi-Fi. I held the dimmed screen low and checked the message.

> **Wire:** *I have eyes in the sky, but still working on administrative access.*

It really had been a piece of cake to get into the security system. Then again, that was more an indictment of the human element than the technology. With a man on the inside, Lock-E didn't have a chance.

That said, the administrative access was what allowed us to manipulate and turn off cameras. Things were complicated without that piece of the puzzle, but we still had an advantage. With the Wire watching the cameras, we knew where and when I'd be seen.

> **Lead:** *Mingling. We're looking at half attendance so far.*

That was good as well. Much of the outdoor security would be heavily focused on the gate and new entrants, leaving us to operate while they were distracted. That benefit only worked in our favor, however, once Cisco and I got past them. I checked in with my status as well.

> **Handler:** *At the front. Will update once inside.*

We settled into position to wait for an opening.

Breach

Getting past guards isn't like most action movies. You can Jason Bourne your way through things if you're an assassin racking up a kill count, but that type of behavior tends to invite lethal retaliation. It was the reason I usually forwent carrying a firearm, tonight being no exception. Cisco might've been close to bulletproof, but I wasn't.

The silent entry of a secret agent is far superior, but even that breaks from the spy-movie mold. Indiscriminately knocking people on the back of their skulls and hoping they stay unconscious for the length of the heist is the definition of poor planning. Most knockouts only last a matter of seconds. Even if the blow keeps them down longer than that, any more than a minute and I'd begin to worry about permanent brain damage.

So the Hollywood hijinks were out.

Then comes the waiting. I like to dig at the boring paperwork, but there's nothing glamorous about hiding under a beverage cart for thirty minutes and then lying in the dirt for another thirty. Intricate plan or no, you still need to wait for your moment. You need a lot of patience in this business, and it's rarely easy. I had to calm Cisco's jitters down twice. He was ready to go, moment or no.

We snuck along the left wall and stopped at the last of the thick bushes, forty feet from the nearest guard. Trees lined the wall all the way past the house, but their cover was thin and well-lit with accent lights. Those spotlights negated Cisco's shadow magic.

The four guards wore dark pants. Their yellow polos were emblazoned with the blue-stitched Lock-E logo and made them easy to spot. They were outfitted with pistols and pepper spray on their belts. Two flanked the table on the right side of the house. This was where guests were being admitted, and where the chance of altercations was highest. This was where your invitation was checked against a list and the pass token collected and placed in a valet cabinet.

The other two guards were stationed at the front door of the Conway House. The one on our right stood before the entry steps while the other watched the door and the left side of the house from his vantage on the grand porch. He overlooked the path we intended to slip down. All told, eight members of the twenty-two-man security team were watching the front of the property, and this was the weakest point of entry. Once we reached the side of the house, the alley between it and the high wall was unguarded.

But that was getting ahead of ourselves. First came the waiting. And the watching. As always, I went over the basics in my head.

Rule number one: no killing. Rule number two: steal only from someone who has it coming. And rule number three: be a professional. Did I have the formula down or what? It was a stupid thing to recount, but it reminded me of more innocent times, when I was a young thief with a father, back when I'd felt invincible.

I huffed. The calming effect of the ritual was negated by me analyzing why I performed it. So I kept counting as I pulled an overeager Cisco away from the brush line. Rule number four: make sure the necromancer doesn't get us all killed.

Finding my center, I paid particular attention to the reactions of the guards and staff to guests and anything unexpected. An argument at the greeting table was quickly smoothed over. A misplaced pass token was dug out of the back seat of a car. Minor misunderstandings were calmly resolved without the diversion we needed. Without our moment. So we waited, counting on a certain class of entitled brat showing up and kicking things off for us.

We weren't disappointed.

A gold patron in a flashy Mercedes attempted to bring in two guests with her plus one. The valet didn't even let them both out of the car. The Lock-E guard at the steps immediately noticed and approached. It was a small opening, but it was there for the taking.

I waved my hand and a large jackrabbit appeared at my side. His eyes were green and possessed human awareness. His coat was a tattered black, his ears were ragged and pointy, his tail was long and winding, like a cat's, and he sat upright.

"Puta madre!" cursed Cisco, recoiling from the animal and the sudden stench of overripe berries. He worked his jaw. "You need to warn me next time you do that."

I smirked. "How're you doing, Puck?"

"Always game, Shyla. If the price is right."

I placed the iron coin of Belial, the archon of his home Erebus, into his little black mitts. He sniffed at it a second and nodded, satisfied.

"Who am I having fun with?" he asked.

We turned to the gold Mercedes. A young woman with too much makeup argued with the valet about bringing in her two friends, both wearing gowns as snazzy and showy as hers. If this had been admission to a nightclub, the three would've been plucked out of line and personally escorted through the front door without the need to even ask. But this wasn't that, and the security team wasn't about to be taken in by a low-cut gown with high-pressed cleavage.

The guard rounded the car, appraising the driver and the three female passengers. His training taught him to avoid the obvious and look for other signs of trickery or threats. I pointed at the other guard watching the left wall.

"See that guy on the porch? I need him looking away from the alley so my friend and I can sneak past. But he can't ever for a moment suspect there's anything unusual. We don't want the whole team going to red alert."

The mangy rabbit scoffed. "Don't take me for an amateur."

He bent to all fours and shook his body like a wet dog, starting from his head and working in stages to his butt. When he was done, he'd nearly doubled in size and changed into the shape of a coyote. From what I'd seen in the past, the animal bordered on the limits of what he could handle. Without further ado, Puck sprang out of the bushes, skirted the Mercedes with a wide berth so he wouldn't be noticed by anyone in the dispute, and headed straight for the front porch.

"You are one creepy biker chick," Cisco muttered.

I grinned. That was probably a compliment, coming from him.

The guard on the porch caught site of the coyote. He did a double-take and looked around. The wild animals were an uncommon sight but did pop their heads up now and then, though they'd usually keep their distance.

The guard reached for his radio but tensed as Puck approached. Instead of making a call, he stepped to the edge of the porch and waved his arms in a threatening manner.

Puck lowered his ears and strafed sideways along the front of the Conway House, away from the guard but straight toward the greeting table.

"Watch it," said the guard, opting to keep the matter off the air. He hurried toward the table as the other guards were alerted to the situation.

The one at the car eyed the scene and turned back to the Mercedes. The gold patron had picked one of her friends to accompany her. The unlucky third guest had to remain in the car, and their driver wasn't given a parking ticket to remain on the grounds. The guard walked down the driveway to follow the car a bit as it descended. He called into his radio to announce their exit from the property.

Meanwhile, Puck veered from the table to change the sight lines. Instead of facing us, the guards all turned toward the driveway.

"Now or never," I said.

With everyone either watching the car or the coyote, we sprinted along the left wall.

"Hold my hand," whispered Cisco.

He grabbed me and I didn't have time to tell him to fuck off, so I went along with it. We darted toward the house. Puck retreated down the driveway, following the car, but stopped and turned for one last look. That hesitation bought us a few more seconds. Unfortunately, the guard in the driveway backed away and turned to check the house again.

Cisco shifted into a mass of black shadow and tugged me. Together we dashed forward, moving the breadth of several yards in an instant, and materialized past the corner of the house. No screams of alert, no messages from the Wire that an alarm was triggered—we had safely made it to the dark alley without being seen. In the distance, Puck released a melancholy howl at his apparent lack of success.

A trickster till the end.

Party Crashers

We snuck alongside the Conway House, sticking to the wall in case a stray guard peeked down our path. There were no doors on this side of the house, and the few sets of large windows were barred with Spanish-style iron. Cisco inspected possible entry points, which I thought was cute. I made my way to the far corner to get eyes on the back lawn.

Once again, it was even more picturesque than the pictures. The wide veranda was constructed of a semi-circle of brick, strong columns lining its diameter. A long bar table covered by a white tablecloth was well attended by staff digging into metal carts of ice cubes. Fancy glassware and bottles lined nearby shelves. The opposite end of the veranda housed buffet tables with trays of appetizers, although wait staff did roam the area passing them out as well.

The great lawn was manicured grass, a soft light-green variety that made the yard feel like an oasis. The centerpiece fountain in the back of the yard accentuated that, but the permanent stage built at its head stuck out like a sore thumb. I could guarantee you, Frank Lloyd Wright was rolling in his grave.

Guests intermingled among the rows of tables. I spotted six Lock-E guards, most of them at the entrance to the indoor lounge. Intel said there were eight in the back, leaving six inside. The few guards on the lawn did a good job of blending with the perimeter. Once you were in the party, they were out of sight, out of mind. No one would be hassled unless they started a fight or attempted to get indoors without proper authorization.

The Lead's bright-red dress stood out as she made her way through the crowd, smiles and laughs creating instant kinship with strangers. She was already making friends, and in fact was hanging off the arm of a dapper young man. Some people were naturals at these things.

The Lead had been briefed on as many attending gold patrons as possible. Her goal was to find someone important and unfamiliar—and hopefully a secret platinum patron. Whenever there was a pretty woman involved, there was usually someone willing to impress her, even if it meant walking her into a restricted area. Sometimes *especially* if it meant that.

It took me an additional minute to spot the Custodian. A half hour into the party and he was waiting alone against a stone column. The man, by his very nature, seemed to be forgotten.

I pulled back to rejoin Cisco.

"None of the windows are open," he murmured. "I don't

think I can get in without breaking anything."

"Have some respect," I said. "This is a historical landmark."

The Conway House was built for show. The first floor had towering ceilings and rested on a hefty foundation, hence the steps for the large front porch. The dramatic sizing positioned the second-floor windows thirty feet above the ground.

"I'm warning you," I said.

He gave me a weird look. "Wha—?"

Bernard puffed in with a cloud of sulfur. Cisco tensed but didn't jump. He was getting better at this. The gargoyle joined me as I studied the second-floor windows.

"That's the one," I said, pointing. "John said it was his father's office."

"On a first-name basis with billionaires, I see," mused Bernard.

"Maybe a one-time billionaire. I doubt he's worth that much now."

"How the mighty have fallen." The gargoyle hopped onto the wall and crept to the window.

The hellion's magic allowed him to grip the stucco without destroying it with his claws. It was why gargoyles were naturals at climbing and standing on the slimmest of precipices, no matter how precarious. I couldn't think of better climbers, only being limited by their size and great weight. There were some places where a squirrel would fare better than a gargoyle.

Bernard climbed down the wall, head right over mine.

171

"The office is empty but the windows are locked."

"That's what I'm for."

I gave him my hand, and Bernard carried me up. I pulled out my picks and worked on the edge of the steel-framed window. It was a solid mechanism, and well built, but it was old and lacked a tight seal. I got my tools in and threw the lock, then pulled the window and squeezed my arm in. It didn't give as much as I'd hoped, but I managed to reach the swing arm and open it. With a rush of satisfaction and nervousness, I stepped inside.

It was only a moment before Bernard retrieved Cisco. Rather than have the gargoyle stomp around on the old wood floors, I unsummoned him for now.

"I feel like Rapunzel," said Cisco, brushing his shoulder.

I shook my head and closed the window. Then I went to my phone.

> **Handler:** *We're inside.*

Cisco snuck to the open door more quietly than I expected from a guy like him. The hall sconces beyond were lit but on a dimmer. I'm sure it added to the ambiance from the first floor looking up. That moody glimpse was all tonight's guests would get of the old home's second story.

The good news was, barring accidental noises on our part, no Lock-E guards would patrol this level of the house. The bad news was the stairways were heavily guarded, both to keep anyone from going up and to ensure proper admission into the basement.

"What now?" asked Cisco.

I moved to a series of framed photographs on the wall and shrugged. "It's the Lead's turn."

"Another distraction?"

"Something like that. Weren't you listening when we went over it?"

"I figured you had it covered."

He joined me in studying the photos. They featured pictures of the Conway family at various public functions. John Sr. receiving the keys to the city. Him and his wife standing at a leveled construction site, which happened to be the same spot we were on now, before the building existed. There were pictures of John and John Jr. together.

"They look like magazine shots," said Cisco.

I nodded. Each probably belonged in a press packet somewhere. The photographs were professionally produced, lacking the candid nature of spontaneous snapshots. Given that, it was difficult to get a feel for father and son. The pictures made no statement about their relationship.

"They used to book public tours through the house," I explained.

"Yeah?" Cisco seemed skeptical. "I don't see the allure of an old house."

"The tours were only for a few hours once a week. I suppose it was a chance to peek inside a better life."

"Better why? Just because some asshole has money? That's not what life's about. Look at this pair. You think this father was joyful about his family? You think this son felt loved?"

I stared blankly at the pictures. My inability to answer hung in the air.

Cisco shook his head. "It doesn't look like it to me."

"So that's it," I said. "Without a happy family, life's worthless?"

He watched me a long moment while he held back a grimace. "I'm sorry, Shyla. I don't know what—" He exhaled forcefully. "Look, if I learned one thing over the last couple years, it's that family's what you make of it."

My phone buzzed. I pulled it from my pocket. "Oh, and here I was thinking you learned that revenge works." I checked the update.

> **Wire:** *I can't confirm the ID of the guest the Lead is with. It's a good indication that he's a platinum member.*
> **Custodian:** *Excellent. See if he can get you inside.*

The Lead would be checking her cell phone and taking selfies as any good socialite would, but at some point too much nosing around on her phone might be suspicious. Our live communication was secure but working on a delay, which only increased the down time.

> **Handler:** *Have you secured admin access?*

> **Wire:** *Not yet. I'm able to monitor the silent alarm, but I can't disable it yet.*
> **Custodian:** What's the problem?
> **Wire:** *Just an unexpected layer of authentication due to me not having a hard line.*
> **Handler:** *Can you crack it?*
> **Wire:** *These guys are good, but I'm better. I'll get inside before the Lead does. Don't worry about my end.*

His assurance didn't relieve me much. The Wire was good at what he did, but what he did was plan ways around security systems. His work required in-depth study, expensive equipment, and inside contacts. He was extremely capable. That said, I sometimes wondered about his ability to think on his feet. To react to unexpected threats in the field. As long as everything went right, the Wire was aces, but I rarely worried about things going right.

> **Lead:** *I'll take you up on that wager. Guess which little lady's visiting the indoor lounge for a drink as we speak?*

I snorted in contempt but couldn't help being impressed. Cisco read over my shoulder.

"You have your own phone," I sassed.

"You mean this?" He pulled out his personal phone.

I glared. "What are you doing with that? You're

supposed to—"

"Don't worry about my burner. I picked it up local so it won't even trace back to Miami."

"I'm worried about you not having a way to contact the team."

"That's what you're for," he said with a smile. "Besides, the Custodian's not gonna keep tabs on my position with a tracker that easily."

I bit down. He wasn't wrong. If I could get around it on the job I would, but it was impossible. Cisco was taking advantage of his free agency. Now it was another complication in my babysitting gig.

"Let's see what we're dealing with," I said and strode out the office door.

The Door Down

We glided across the wood floor in the hall, doing our best to minimize creaks. The large planks of redwood, now very illegal, held up admirably. A turn in the hall led to a Victorian banister overlooking a lively indoor lounge. An oval bar was fully attended by guests and staff and, true to her word, the Lead mingled among the VIPs with an air of sophistication.

Her date was a handsome man, a little thin but above-average height. I wondered what his intentions with her were, and then I wondered if he was human. It was our job, as a team, to protect the Lead, who often had to very publicly insert herself into the center of the action.

We continued down the hallway. As long as we stayed below the light line of the upward-facing sconces, we were invisible. The overlook ended and the hall closed with walls on either side before the high ceiling once again opened up over the first floor. This time the banister led down a grand stairway in the center of the house. A single guard stood at the bottom, facing away from us. The area was otherwise empty.

Before I could move into the opening, a few voices came from the bar. A man and two women strolled into view, following our same path but on the first floor. Cisco pulled me backward.

"Those are the jinns I saw at Helping Home."

My focus sharpened. At first glance they appeared completely normal, but Cisco was right about there being something off about them. The women's necks were too long, the man's shoulders too wide. They looked like people but their features were a little too exaggerated, a little too perfect. Their attire was relatively spartan considering. Gray business suits all around, with one of the women opting for a skirt and pink heels. They spoke amongst themselves and passed into the adjoining room without so much as a nod to the guard.

After my talk with John Conway's man, I knew the layout of the house and where the jinns were heading. Once the coast was clear, I led Cisco past the stairway. The corridor narrowed again before opening up to another overlook that mirrored the opposite side of the house, except instead of a bustling lounge this was a homey sitting room. No one was relaxing here and the jinns had already gone below.

There were no stairs to the second floor, but the inside wall of the sitting room featured a slim staircase going down. The only two people present were the Lock-E guards in their bright yellow shirts.

"What do you think?" asked the heavyset black man. He was bald and looked like he could lift a table.

"The blonde," said the white guard. "Definitely."

"You crazy, man. Ain't no way I'm getting with a woman in slacks."

The other man scoffed. "Hey, I'm a sucker for skirts too, but the blonde had a prettier face."

In the absence of apparent guests, the guards spoke as openly and casually about them as if they were debating fantasy football rosters.

Cisco hiked a shoulder and nodded in agreement. "It was her lips," he agreed. "You see those things?"

I rolled my eyes *hard*.

"That's 'cause you haven't learned," said the big guard. "When the lights go out, I ain't looking at no faces, but a girl who can't put on a skirt don't know how to move in the bedroom. Believe that."

I glared at Cisco and dared him to add additional commentary. He shifted uncomfortably.

The guards ceased their conversation as more guests arrived. My eyes widened as the Lead came into view on the arm of the dapper gentleman.

"She moves fast," I muttered. In this case, it was a little too fast.

"Hello sir," said the big man. The other guard produced a retinal scanner and held it to the guest's eye. When they were done, he moved to scan the Lead.

"She's with me," said the man firmly.

"May I?" asked the guard with the scanner. The

gentleman nodded and the guard asked the Lead to lift her arms. He actually patted her down. "Your phone, ma'am."

The Lead turned to her date and then back to the guard. "Is that really necessary?"

"It is, ma'am, if you want to go down. No cameras allowed."

The gentleman urged her with a firm nod, and the Lead surrendered her phone to the guard. The white guy stepped aside and the black guy led them down the steps. I crept toward the banister to watch them descend and the Lead's eyes caught mine for a split second.

I had to hold back a moment until the guard at the top of the steps looked away. I stood and leaned over to see directly below. The big guard typed a code into a keypad that unlocked the door, but I didn't catch it in time. The guests stepped in and I backed away as the door closed.

I retreated to the hallway with a curse. It had happened so fast there wasn't anything I could've done. I sat against the wall and typed on my phone.

> **Handler:** *The basement door is coded. The Lead's already inside.*
> **Wire:** *That's not in the security report.*
> **Handler:** *Neither was the fact that they're taking phones from guests. The Lead's disconnected.*

I huffed in frustration, but I wasn't surprised the Wire's Lock-E contact didn't have all the details. The guards themselves weren't allowed in the basement. As far as we knew, they weren't apprised of the subterranean and supernatural aspects of this site. The basement was a private party for rich muckety-mucks and their whores.

What did surprise me was that John Conway's man hadn't mentioned the door code either. If Lock-E wasn't responsible then maybe it was a retrofit by Helping Home.

> **Custodian:** *We need to get in there.*
> **Wire:** *Working on it.*

I steadied myself with a breath. The Lead's job was never completely safe, but right now she was behind a locked and guarded door, in the presence of who knows how many supernatural creatures. She must've been out of her mind.

It was a few tense minutes before the Wire got back to us.

> **Wire:** *I snagged admin access. I can unlock the basement door without the alarm going off, but I need to do it right before you need it. Otherwise security might notice it's disabled and go on alert. I can keep it open for just under sixty seconds before the automatic alarm goes off, so don't call it until you need it. I'm ready on your word.*

I winced.

> **Handler:** *That's going to be a problem. The guards were suspicious of the Lead. She couldn't get her distraction off. I'm stuck outside.*
> **Custodian:** *Figure it out, Handler. We might have one shot at this.*

I gritted my teeth and held back as more guests wandered in.

"The shadow can carry us to the floor without a sound," whispered Cisco. "If the guards are looking the other way..."

I didn't like it. We could get down and get the door unlocked, but we wouldn't escape notice opening and closing the door. Not without something bigger.

It was unfortunate because the bigger the distraction, the more unnatural, thus the more likely it was to blow the entire job. But that extreme case was better than being caught red-handed trying to sneak past a guard. That would endanger the job and my health at the same time.

The Lock-E detail let two men into the basement while I summoned Bernard. I explained the situation and he quietly climbed to the ceiling. Knocking down the sitting room's large chandelier was sure to be a huge distraction. In an old house, it might even be waved away. We just had to make sure the gargoyle didn't get noticed in the process.

I typed into the chat...

> **Handler:** *Do it now.*

... But I held off on sending it. I wouldn't until the right moment.

The two guards were alone again. I nodded to Bernard and he made his way across the ceiling. Cisco and I crept toward to banister and held hands, ready to pounce.

"Now *that* girl..." said the heavyset guard, hearkening back to the Lead. "She's the type with a pretty face who I *know* can work it in the bedroom."

The other one laughed. "You gotta watch out with those, brother. They'll squeeze you dry."

"I could use a little squeezing, if you know what I mean."

Something moved in the shadows below us. There was a wisp, not unlike Cisco's shadow magic, but it solidified into the form of a cloaked figure.

"You seeing this?" asked Cisco.

Bernard was working on a heavy screw at the base of the chandelier. I put my hand up to signal him to stop.

Cisco was as tense as a mousetrap. "What is that thing?"

The smell of rotten wine wafted up. "Nothing good."

As the two men chatted, the ghostly hellion sprang on the back of the large one. I flinched but the demon was completely unnoticed, giving the guard a bear hug from behind.

"Are you doing this?" spat Cisco.

"It's not me."

He eyed Bernard, just in case I was lying.

The black man started another sentence but paused. He worked his shoulder and put his hand to his chest, then tried again. He couldn't speak.

"What's the matter? For once you don't have something

to say?" asked his coworker.

The struggling man rapped his chest with a fist. What I first thought was a sleeper hold started looking like a heart attack. The man cried out and collapsed to the floor.

The other guard spoke into his radio. "Condition Orange. James is down at Door Zero." He crouched to check his friend. The cloaked demon backed away and vanished. Lock-E guards stormed the room. I banished Bernard and retreated from the banister.

"What happened?" they asked.

"I don't know," stammered the guard. "We were just talking and then he fell."

"Was he hit with something?"

"I'm telling you, we were alone. And we ate the same food and I feel fine. I think it's his heart."

A few guests strolled into the room. The new guards kept them at bay. One of them called for an ambulance. The quiet sitting room was turning into a spectacle.

My phone buzzed.

Custodian: *Open the door.*

Behind the collecting crowd, my boss stepped into the room and adjusted his wire frames. He moved slowly, unconcerned with the frantic activity around him. Strangely, everyone was also unconcerned with him. It was almost as if they didn't know he was there. Just like the cloaked demon, the others couldn't see him.

The Custodian seemed to glow ever so slightly as he

stepped over the dying man and went down the stairs. If he knew where I was, he didn't wait for me. The door was unlocked and he slipped inside.

"Damn," I said under my breath. "That gives us less than a minute. We need to get in that door."

"Back away a moment please," called one of the roving guards. "Admittance to the basement is suspended for the next five minutes. Please return to the lounge or the banquet outside."

The guard herded guests away, who did their best to stay and peek.

"Let's get him outside," urged one of the Lock-E employees. It took three of them to lift the flailing man. They carried him out as the room began to clear.

That was it. The original guard left at the steps and the others temporarily away on urgent business. I had no doubt they'd quickly return to assess the situation. They would consider any further deviation from normal as suspicious. If we were getting inside the basement, it was now or never.

Cisco and I vaulted over the railing and fell straight down into the recessed stairwell. His spellcraft carried us through the shadow and set us gently on the carpeted steps. I held the door open as he slipped inside, and I shut it behind us. We had made it into the basement without being seen.

So far, so good.

I hoped.

The Underground

We found ourselves in a tunnel of rough stone. Soft yellow light painted everything in a warm pallor. There was no sign of the Custodian.

"What the hell was that?" growled Cisco.

"Keep your voice down," I snapped back. "We're behind enemy lines here."

His face burned in anger and he stomped around, but he managed to control his volume. "Did your team just kill that guy?"

"I don't know. It was a hellion. If I had to guess, the Custodian used the Ring of Solomon to improvise."

"So it wasn't part of the plan?"

"I'm not a killer. I doubt you can make the same claim."

His face contorted into a snarl, but he didn't bite back. I'd hoped the comment would stave him off. What surprised me was the flash of guilt in his eyes. I supposed everybody had their secrets. Now wasn't the time to deal with them.

I pushed ahead. It was only a few yards until we reached

a thick steel door that was open. It reminded me of a bank vault, and believe me I've seen a few of those, except this one was designed to slide open and shut by receding into the wall. It was dusty and didn't show signs of recent use.

"This place must've been built to be a bunker," I noted.

Cisco grimaced at the thick door. "It's enchanted."

I took a closer look and saw the protective runes etched into the metal. I kicked dirt off the steel track in the floor and saw more of the same. "Hellions can't cross this line."

"Good," he said with a snort.

I wasn't so easily comforted. Was this barrier meant to keep hellions out, or keep them in?

Past the door, the tunnel widened into a modest foyer with several freestanding clothes racks. We were greeted with hanger after hanger of identical cloaks. They were dark crimson, with the texture of velour and a hem of brass.

Cisco chuckled. "Are these guys serious?"

"Probably overly so. The cloaks are stupid but they're perfect." I picked out a smaller one and slipped it over my jacket, pulling it shut and drawing the hood over my head. "What do you think, platinum patron or cat burglar?"

"You're something all right."

We were interrupted by a snort. I jumped to attention, reaching into my jacket for my ASP. Just within the continuing tunnel, a man rested against the wall, snoring.

"The Custodian's pulling out all his tricks tonight," commented Cisco as he grabbed his own cloak and slipped it on.

It made me wonder what else the angel could do. It

wasn't a pleasing thought because it just led to me fearing I was in over my head. Cisco entered the tunnel and I kept pace, pretending to have his confidence. The passage descended slowly.

Neither of us were familiar with convocations. I was beginning to bet they were steeped in ritual, though. The robes were classic secret-society fare.

"So what's the plan down here?" he asked.

"We need to find the Lead."

"I mean about the scepter."

I pondered that a moment, eyes forward as the sound of laughter fluttered down the hall. "Simple. We find those jinns of yours. Have them give a warning to the shah. Blame his abrupt exit on an emergency in his kingdom or whatever."

The tunnel opened into a large lounge with a high ceiling, impressive since we were underground. Thirty guests sat on wide couches, beds, or made their rounds at a corner bar holding colorful cocktails with bubbling contents and wafts of smoke.

Every single person in the room, even the service staff, wore crimson robes, many with hoods drawn but not all. Aside from the theatrics, nothing appeared spectacular. Blending in was going to be a breeze. Unfortunately, that meant it might be difficult to locate the jinns and the Lead.

"Ha!" said Cisco, sidling up to a large photograph in an ornate frame. "That's a picture they don't show on the tour."

It was a black-and-white portrait of John Conway Sr.

standing regal in his crimson robe. A label along the bottom read "Sargon."

"It's like a bad 70s sci-fi villain," he joked.

"Sixties," I corrected. "*Star Trek.*"

He looked at me funny. "I was kidding."

"It's also an ancient Akkadian name. Sargon the Great was the first emperor in the world."

"Okay, I'm sorry I brought it up."

He turned his attention to the party while I studied the portrait a little longer. For all its pretense, it was a far more honest picture of John Sr. than the ones in his office. This was a man who thought himself great. And maybe one who wanted to change the world.

"The jinns aren't here," said Cisco.

I assessed the crowd of cloaked figures. "And how could you possibly know that?"

He shook his head. "They were too serious for this. Everyone here is drinking and having a grand-old time. Those jinns were on business." He pointed to a passage in the far wall. "I think they went that way. And so did your boss."

The exit was a central feature of the lounge, as if we were in the lobby and beyond was the theater. I didn't doubt his instincts in this case.

"I still need to find the Lead," I said. "If it was me, I'd stay in here where it's relatively safe."

"You do that," he said, backing towards the exit. "I'm Cisco Suarez, and danger's my middle name, so I'm going this way."

"No, you're sticking with me."

"Am I though?" Despite asking the question, he winked, flipped around, and stomped off.

"Don't you dare." I followed him a step but stopped. "Ugh!" I couldn't abandon the Lead due to Cisco's recklessness, even if I didn't like her. Hell, I wasn't sure which of the two I liked least. All I could do was hurry.

I strolled around the room, checking the guests. A good deal of them were silvans who tended to be shorter than me. I could discount them outright. As for the taller ones, I could make out their faces even under the hood. I simply needed to pretend to be interested in their boisterous conversations from time to time. I heard mention of a royal wedding, talk of nymphs and minotaurs, murder and intrigue. I even heard mention of a necromancer, and I deeply hoped they weren't referring to Cisco. The last thing this heist needed was a member everyone would recognize.

My phone buzzed, and I snatched it eagerly before realizing it might not be allowed. While the Lead's had been confiscated, I wasn't sure if proper platinum patrons were allowed the luxury. Regardless, not a single person was snapping pictures of their drinks or settling arguments on Google. I nestled into a remote corner and peeked at the phone under my cloak.

Custodian: *I trust you made it inside, Handler?* **Handler:** *Yes.*

> **Custodian:** *Excellent. Our first prerogative is confirming the shah is in attendance. Let me know as soon as you locate him.*
> **Handler:** *I need to find the Lead first.*
> **Custodian:** *Leave it. This job's too important. She knows the risks.*

I put my phone away and leaned against the wall. I wanted to find the jinns too, and even though my reasons were more altruistic, I couldn't focus on the scepter if the Lead was in danger. I didn't bother messaging the Custodian with my objection. He would see any hesitation as weakness. He would use it against me.

That didn't mean I was going to abandon her.

I continued my lap around the bar, checking everyone in attendance. It was impossible to catch every face while still remaining subtle, but it was easy enough to rule out any of them being the Lead. There was a good chance she'd gone further into the basement with her dapper gentleman as a guide. I just hoped she knew what she was doing.

"May I?"

A man in a cloak took my hand and pulled me into a dance. He spun me into a pirouette before settling his palm on my side, unbothered by the lack of actual music to step to. His face pulled close to mine. It was Asmodeus.

"Ah," he crooned, "the pleasures of the flesh. Act natural."

I stiffened against his body, which excited him all the

more. "How'd you get past the wards at the door?"

His fingers rapped wantonly on my hip. "Don't fret about such minor details."

I glanced around the lounge. Nobody took note of the two crazy people sharing a slow dance without a song.

"You're doing an admirable job watching the new team member," he said drily.

I lifted my chin. "And apparently you're watching us in turn."

"Ah, but you're a grown woman, Shyla, of sound mind and body. What a fabulous mind you have." He pulled me tight. "And what a maddening body." The demon pressed into me. He was hungry and wanting and strong. "It's a shame we're both here on business," he sighed, "but the scepter waits for neither man nor woman nor angel. Have you figured out what it is yet?"

"A symbol of power."

"No... No, no, no." The hellion extended his arm to separate us before pulling me close. "Have you ever known our mutual boss to be concerned with mere symbols?"

I gritted my teeth. "So it has power, then. Does it have something to do with Sargon the Akkadian?"

Asmodeus showed his teeth in a genuine laugh. "That one's a nickel short of being a prophet, don't you think? No, Sargon's loyalties are a little ancient, don't you think? It's the newer players that come on strongest. If that weren't the case, power would never change hands."

"And you'd still be a king," I taunted. His expression tightened, but I didn't revel in my wordplay.

Asmodeus was referring to Christianity. It was obvious by the disdain in his voice and the scowl on his face. "Eventually," he said with determination, "there comes a time when a line is drawn in the sand, a literal Parting of the Sea. That is a moment there is no going back from. Once certain beings wield certain power, everything changes."

I stopped the dance mid stride, still holding the demon's hand. "You don't want the Custodian getting his hands on the scepter either, do you?"

"Have I said that?" he asked with feigned innocence. "I could never go against my master's wishes. Yet I can reveal this much. The scepter has been in responsible hands for thousands of years. You might wonder why that is so."

A lilted laugh caught my attention. For a moment I'd hoped it was the Lead working her mark, but I wasn't so lucky. It was a plump woman with two suitors.

"Where's the Lead?" I asked Asmodeus.

His face contorted. "How is that important?"

"Where is she?"

He hiked a shoulder. "I'd wager she's either having the time of her life, or the conclusion to it."

I jerked my hand from his and squared up to him, uninterested in continuing this charade.

He watched me a moment before deflating. "I never can say no to you, my dear. The silvan took her down the left passage. I don't think that one has her best interests at heart. But take my advice and go down the right."

I strode to the rear exit. It wasn't guarded, and it appeared I was the only operator who hadn't pressed on yet.

"I must warn you," said Asmodeus, scrambling to follow. "I cannot help you."

"I don't need your help."

He grabbed my arm. "You might. Your usual methods will be hampered."

I jerked my arm but he held on tight. "Asmodeus," I growled a little too loudly, "you better—"

A man behind the bar snapped at us. "Is that guy bothering you?" he asked sharply.

His hood drew open enough for me to identify him. It was John Conway's butler, on the service staff.

Asmodeus scurried away before causing a scene. I turned back, ready to nod thanks to the butler, but he had already moved to the other side of the bar.

Great, we were being watched by someone else. Who *didn't* have a stake in this convocation?

I pushed into the tunnel, stifling the curse on my lips. I wasn't sure who else was down here listening.

Down the Rabbit Hole

I grumbled and moved ahead. The main corridor featured brighter lights and echoes of congregated voices. Despite my demonic advice, I veered down a leftward tunnel that resembled a mine shaft, with rough rock walls and a single line of electrical lights hanging on one side.

I began to realize how large the basement of the Conway House was. The property sat central on a large mountain plateau. Rather than being just a few underground rooms, this was an entire tunnel network in the hills. For all I knew, some of it was older than the house itself.

It made me once again ponder new powers and old. What had Asmodeus been getting at with his roundabout advice? How was I supposed to figure out what the scepter was when he told me nothing about it?

Harsh voices ahead ended my speculation. Two men, and the Lead with them. I was relieved Asmodeus hadn't led me astray, though I began to fear the need for such a remote location. The passage had doorways into several small rooms. The chambers were plain, spartanly furnished, and ideal for a little alone time.

"I need to get back to the ceremony," came a voice. "Do with her what you will."

I ducked into an empty room as a figure stepped into my tunnel. Though the hall had a line of lights, the room was unlit. I pressed to the wall and waited as the man hurried by. It was the Lead's date. He must've known who she was and lured her here. When he was gone I peeked my head out.

"But why?" asked the Lead.

I tiptoed down the tunnel toward their room.

"Why do you think?" snarled a voice I recognized. "You thought you could take advantage of me and get away with it?"

"We didn't hurt you."

"You put my life in danger."

I reached the doorway of the dark room. The silvan diplomat from the Puzzle Box held a knife toward the Lead. She was backed against the wall, trapped. She wore a cloak, as her date did, but the diplomat didn't. Behind them, a wide stairway led another level down.

The Lead swallowed. "What are you, exactly?"

The silvan smiled. "There'll be plenty of time to enjoy my true form once we go down the rabbit hole." He offered his hand. "Come peacefully."

"I won't." The Lead bit down defiantly. "I'll tell. Remember, you don't want your people knowing it was you who told us about this place."

"Watch your threats, or you might convince me to gut

you right here."

I stepped into the room. "That would be the quickest way to end your life," I announced.

He spun. "You too. I knew it."

"Put the knife down."

His eyes narrowed. "What are you doing here? What do you want with the convocation?"

I took another step toward him. "That's not your concern. I told you to drop it. You still can. We all go our separate ways and no one needs to bat an eye."

"You want me to drop it?" returned a hard voice. "You may be assassins. My king's life may be in danger."

"We're not here for the silvans," I promised. "You and your kind have nothing to fear from us."

His eyes narrowed. "Who are you then? What does a hellion summoner want with our convocation?"

"I guess it's gonna keep you up at night." I looked over the Lead. "How're you doing?"

"Happy to see you." She came off the wall and headed toward me.

The silvan brandished his knife. I waved my arm to call Bernard. The motion felt empty as there was no resistance against my fingers.

The silvan shoved the Lead against the wall. "Not so fast." He turned to me trying to tickle the air. "Your magicks don't work down here, summoner. Convocations are warded against your evil."

I unzipped my jacket and pulled out my stun gun, holding it in the fold of the cloak. It was an older model than the one I'd lost at the Puzzle Box, and I wasn't entirely confident wielding it. "Let her go."

"It's not happening," he spat. He motioned to the stairs. "I'm taking her with me, to the Nether. You'll stay up here if you value your life."

He moved for the steps and I pounced, zapping him with a surge of electricity. The charge went through him and the Lead. They both tripped to the ground, but neither were incapacitated.

"You bitch."

The silvan swept my legs out. He was scrawny but a lot stronger than he looked. I landed hard. Another blow knocked my weapon from my hands. He crawled over me and snarled.

"Maybe I'll take you with me too."

The Lead plunged his knife into his back. His eyes went wide. I rolled away as he collapsed, recovering my weapon. The Lead and I backed away with wide eyes.

"He's dead," she said.

I swallowed. He definitely wasn't getting back up. "It's okay," I said after a minute. "He was going back down anyway. He's not wearing a cloak. He wasn't part of the convocation. Nobody will miss him."

"But if anybody..."

"I'll handle it."

I grabbed his legs and dragged him to the stairs, peering into the blackness below. This wasn't an ordinary staircase. A few steps into the rock and all color winked out. A tingle of magic crackled as I neared. The rabbit hole to the Nether was right here.

I took a breath and pulled the body down...

And landed in a foggy dirt tunnel. Ambient light wafted through the mist. A few crab-like creatures skittered at my sudden arrival. I scanned up and down the tunnel. No sign of anyone. Beside me, a wide opening in the wall led back up, this time fading into dull light.

I dragged the dead silvan some way down the passage. Eyes and antennae perked at my passing, and the blue crabs followed. It was gross, but the scourgelings were doing me a favor. I found a clump of them in a wide alcove and I dropped the body in. The crabs chittered excitedly at the fresh meat. I retreated with a grimace.

I hadn't killed the silvan, but this felt like a line crossed. The point of no return. Was I destined to be a killer after all, or would I continue to trifle with stun guns?

I shut the feeling down. I didn't enjoy the feeling of helplessness, but I wouldn't give in to the easy path. I'd made a choice a long time ago and I was sticking to it. I didn't blame the Lead for what she'd done, but it hadn't been my hand that had wielded the knife.

I gathered my resolve at the base of the steps. Before I lifted my boot, an inkling came to me. Perhaps the warded tunnels of the Conway House prevented me from reaching the World Below, but I was no longer on the Material Plane. A few steps into a rabbit hole was miles apart from home. The Intrinsics bled through my fingers upon my command. A blast of sulfur exploded from the darkness and my favorite gargoyle was at my side.

"What did I miss?" he asked.

I caught him up and brought him back through to my world. Bernard freely entered the basement tunnel, unhampered by any hellion wards, just as Asmodeus had been. I might not be able to summon him back once he left, but for now the band was back together.

"What's this?" he asked, smelling at the corner of the dark room and producing his find: a large ebony feather.

I blinked. "Does that look like a black owl feather to you?"

"It does. And it has the stink of Hell on it too."

I clenched my jaw. Apparently I wasn't the only one using the Nether loophole to bring a hellion to the convocation.

First Contact

The Lead peeked out the door, eager to leave the scene of the crime. "No one's outside. We might be okay."

I nodded. "We're still in business, so to speak."

"I don't have my phone. The Custodian must be worried about me. Is he here?"

I sighed and framed my statement carefully. "He's... not your friend. I hope you know that."

She gave a defensive snort. "I know. I'm not dumb. But he's our coordinator so he looks out for us."

"He told me not to come for you."

A hard line formed in her brow. I wondered just how well she knew him.

"There's something else. Bedrock's down here too."

That perked her attention. If only she knew the truth about the pair, the continuing charade, but for now the thought of our demonic boss going on a job with us was enough to convince her that this heist was anything but business as usual.

She brushed her straight hair behind her shoulder. "Why would—"

"I probably shouldn't be telling you this," I said, "but we can't let them get the scepter. It's some kind of holy artifact, some kind of portent of power. I know you don't trust me or probably even like me, but bad things are gonna happen if we go through with this job."

She stared at me and I realized my heart was racing. I had just put myself out there, at her mercy. I immediately wished I could take it back.

The Lead scanned the steps to the rabbit hole with a frown. There was some blood left on the ground. When her eyes returned to me, they carried a vulnerability I'd never seen before. "We can't go against Bedrock," she said softly.

"He'll never know. All we need to do is get word to the shah before the convocation starts."

"It's starting now."

"Then we need to hurry. Look, I'm doing this one way or the other. You don't need to be involved."

She took a steadying breath. "My asshole date showed me the antechamber. I'll take you there."

And just like that we were pattering through the tunnel. Instead of going all the way back to the beginning, the Lead turned down an intermediate hall that she must've taken on the way here. I marched at her side while Bernard slunk through the shadows a short distance behind.

At one point the tunnel transitioned to a wood floor. Plaster coated the walls and ceiling, and the lighting changed from a loose wire to permanent fixtures. The Lead paused in a small intersection, walked to a door, stopped, and walked to another one.

"This is the one," she said, inching it open.

The next room was a long hall starting from our right and heading to our left. There were no light fixtures, which was odd for such a large space. The architecture of the central hallway was simple and wide, able to fit ten people across, and lined with stone columns on each side every fifteen feet. Several yards of clearance cushioned the pillars from the outer walls, giving us room to watch without obstructing the path.

"My chaperone called this the black hall. It leads to the white room."

She pointed, but she didn't need to. To our left, two hundred feet down, was an arched doorway with light so intense it was pure white. I recalled John Conway mentioning some kind of purification ritual.

First, we don the cloaks to become nameless. Then we travel through the dark to strip our minds clean. The white room was the last step before the divination chamber.

"Have you been down there?" I asked.

She shook her head. "He said I wasn't allowed. He brought me here to stick his tongue down my throat before selling me out to his Nether friend."

We quieted as a throng of cloaked figures entered the black hall on our right. They were coming from the lounge, which meant the Lead had been right: the convocation was imminent if not already underway.

The area was dark and we were disguised in our cloaks.

With Bernard waiting just outside the side door, we wouldn't attract attention even if we were seen.

The towering columns, high ceiling, and darkness combined to create a reverent atmosphere. The platinum patrons proceeded with careful gaits and respectful whispers when silence wouldn't do. Many kept their heads down. I'd seen enough rituals to understand the black hall and white room served as meditative preludes to a greater ceremony.

A text message broke the spell. It was from Cisco.

"I'm in the convocation room. The shah's here, but surrounded by his guards. No sign of the Custodian."

My lips tightened. This message didn't use our encrypted app, though it was outside the expected channel. Even if the Custodian could eavesdrop, the message didn't overtly signify our betrayal. If questioned about it later, we could still claim to have followed orders. Which meant I had to follow suit.

"People are still streaming in," I responded. "I'll look for another opening."

The Lead leaned over and whispered in my ear. "There they are. You see?"

She pointed to a woman in a cloak. Between the darkness and the hood, I didn't recognize her until spotting the pink heels.

"One of the jinns."

The Lead nodded.

"I need to talk to her." I started forward but she held me back with a smile.

"Not so fast, Handler. You know the score. I'm the lead

on this."

I rolled my eyes. "You don't need to—"

"Relax. I have it under control. Before my date went full psycho, he introduced me to her."

I pulled back and watched her in complete surprise as she strolled out to the jinn. There was no scam, no hijinks, no trick. The Lead simply told a joke that got a laugh and waved the jinn over. They excused themselves, lagged away from the throng, and came to greet me.

"This is the friend I was telling you about," explained the Lead. "She has something important to tell you."

I eyed the cloaked figures parading down the black hall. It surprised me how many attendees there were. "Not here," I said, stepping back through the side door into the smaller tunnel.

The jinn came through and lowered her hood. "That's far enough. I need to know who you are."

We lowered our hoods to match suit, and Bernard was wise enough to remain out of sight.

"First," I said, addressing the Lead, "you've done your part. It's time for you to get out of here."

Her face flushed. "No way. You saved my life. I can help you."

"You already did."

"Stop underestimating me."

"It has nothing to do with that. You need to go before you lose plausible deniability. If anything happens to me, you act like you had no idea I was going against the script. You got it?"

The mention of possible consequences ruffled her composure. "What about the Custodian? I can't leave without him."

"He can handle himself. Trust me. Your job is done. Leave the basement, pick up your phone, enjoy a catered dinner, and wait for us topside."

She licked her lips. Though she wanted to help, her desire for escape handily won out. "Fine. Good luck." Then she nodded at the jinn. "Love your shoes." The Lead headed down the side tunnel where she was unlikely to encounter resistance on the way out.

The jinn continued to eye me suspiciously. She wore her hair in a stark pony tail, and Cisco had been right about her features being exaggerated. She had cheekbones like a cartoon of a supermodel.

"Am I to believe this is some covert operation?" she demanded.

I nodded. "We can't tell you our names, but we were hired to rob the shah."

She sniggered. "That's preposterous. The mere suggestion of a human robbing his most high is beyond credulity."

"Yet it's why we're here. Ask yourself what humans are doing at this convocation. How I know you picked up the brass bell token Friday afternoon."

Her eyes narrowed. "You're here for the staff."

"The golden scepter," I corrected, finding it curious Asmodeus had made the same reference.

The jinn watched me with a curious expression until her

entire posture relaxed. "You don't know what it is."

"What is it?"

"Why do you want it if you don't know?" she returned.

"I don't, but someone does. Someone not of my world or yours. I'm just a hired hand."

"Then why tell me?"

She didn't know what to make of me yet, and I didn't blame her. "Don't you get it? You have access to the shah. He's inside, isn't he?"

She paused a beat before wordlessly nodding.

"You can get word to him. I can't." I splayed my hands out as if everything was as simple as that.

She thought over my meaning for a second. Bernard suddenly growled. The jinn's eyes shot to the darkness, wary. She backed through the doorway, receding into the black hall.

"Wait," I pleaded, "you don't understand." I angrily waved the gargoyle off.

"This is treason!" she spat. "Against your own kind!"

She spun around and crashed right into the hands of the Custodian. Her body flashed with blue energy but his flashed with fire. I dove aside as he shoved her back into the tunnel. She barely screamed before being engulfed by flames and fizzling out into embers.

Abaddon turned to me slowly, the Ring of Solomon orange with heat. His gray eyes were about as cold as I'd ever seen them.

"What were you talking to her about?"

Bernard was close at hand, and I now knew the reason

for his growl. Still, his presence did nothing to help me. Not against the might of an angel. An open palm at my back urged him away. It wasn't easy to fool Abaddon, but right now his anger was directed toward me.

"I was..." I swallowed, unable to hide my nerves. "I was pressing her for information."

The angel's face was stark. "Information."

"She was interested in making a deal."

"You were warned not to make deals with jinns, Shyla."

I shrugged, desperately trying to play off my betrayal. "It's the only way to finish the job. The shah's already in the divination chamber. He's surrounded by bodyguards. I saw an opening..." I petered off and straightened, suddenly indignant. "Why are you hassling me?"

"The shah," he muttered, easing his focus on me. "He's a slippery one, but if he's in there, we've got him." He pulled out his phone and started typing.

"We should wait till the ceremony's complete. Maybe his security detail backs off on his way out."

"No worries on that account," he pronounced. The Custodian hit send on his message and my phone buzzed. Since he wasn't telling me what he wrote, I was forced to check my phone right next to him.

> **Custodian:** *Wire, the shah is here. Lock us down.*

I searched his face, but he was too stoic to even wear a smirk. "What are we locking down?" I asked. "This wasn't part of the plan."

"It was part of my plan, Shyla. A little extra motivation for the team. Right about now, the Wire is overriding the basement's security door. We're locked inside the vault."

I blinked uncertainly. "But why?"

"Because jinns can slip away in a snap if they reach open air. As long as that vault door is shut, the scepter can't escape us. No one goes in or out until we complete the job. And I mean *no one*."

His amusement grew at my stunned expression. "Yes, you know what this means, don't you? There'll be consequences if you don't get that scepter, Shyla. We're all in this one together. Either you get that scepter or we all die trying, because there's no going back from here."

Black and White

The Custodian's icy glare didn't lay off me for a second. I wasn't sure if he suspected my true motives or if he outright knew them. Either way, he was having fun torturing me. Despite the explosive tension between us, he calmly went about managing another day in the office. More mind games.

"Well, Handler, what are you waiting for? There's one direction this job is taking you. It's in there." He pointed into the black hall.

I pushed inside if only to put some distance between us. "Aren't you coming?"

"I can't just yet."

His voice seemed to catch as he said it, as if the statement was uncomfortable or an admission of weakness. It made me wonder again why the bearer of the Ring of Solomon, the master of jinnkind, needed someone like me to pull off this job. Couldn't he just waltz right into the divination chamber and demand the scepter?

But I wasn't sure how to use that information yet. Just as I wasn't sure why Asmodeus didn't want Abaddon to be successful here. I was a mere human in this game, and my crisis of conscience didn't involve metaphorical angels and demons on my shoulders. My angels and demons were real, and they'd kill me in a second if I made the wrong decision.

The Custodian followed me into the hall, looking the unassuming administrator again. He was the only one strolling the underground in plainclothes, though I doubted most were able to see him. He made for the entrance back toward the lounge, and pointed to his head in reminder. "Don't forget the hood," he snickered.

I hid my face and idled the opposite way, purposely keeping my stride slow. Thirty seconds later he was gone, and I was the only person in the black hall. Bernard peeked his head in.

"Coast's clear," I told him.

He groaned and rejoined me. "That was closer than usual, even for you."

"Tell me about it."

I withdrew my phone. With the Custodian being so on top of things, I didn't dare warn Cisco about the news. We were on thin enough ice as it was. Instead, I sent a message on the team's encrypted channel.

> **Handler:** *Lead, did you make it out?*

As we trudged toward the white room, I realized we were on an upward trajectory, which was strange seeing as how we were heading deeper into the basement. I wondered if it was some sort of symbolism. We forge ahead, in the dark, striving up towards the light.

Instead of enlightenment, my frown grew as the seconds dragged on. If the Lead had made it past the vault door, she would've recovered her phone and answered by now. The absence of a reply meant she was trapped down here with the rest of us.

> **Handler:** *Wire, the Lead didn't make it out. Open the door for a minute until she gives the okay.*
> **Wire:** *That's a negative, Handler. Give her time. She'll make it.*
> **Handler:** *It's not a matter of making it. We don't need her down here anymore. Let her back topside.*

The Custodian butted into our chat.

> **Custodian:** *The door will stay closed until I give the word. We all have our parts to play.*

I huffed. As we neared the archway ahead, so much light spilled into the room that there was a glare on my phone screen. Using the same app, I sent a private message to the Wire, so only the two of us could talk.

> **Handler:** *Just do it, Wire. Let her out. She almost died down here.*

He must've mulled it over because his response took a full minute.

> **Wire:** *Sorry, no can do. I'm following orders. You will too if you know what's smart.*

I slammed the phone into my pocket. Even what little good I accomplished by saving the Lead was in doubt.

I stopped at the archway as my eyes adjusted to the brightness. We must've been the only stragglers because no one was left in the black hall or, as I confirmed when my vision cleared, the next chamber either.

The white room was a large rectangular space, not as long as the black hall but more impressive. It stood a full two stories, which explained why the previous hall included an upward climb. A full wraparound balcony overlooked a bottom floor with intricate handmade tiles. The ceiling was painted with a wall-to-wall mural that easily passed for a Renaissance piece. The center was the sun, and figures all around reached up, drawn toward it. Some were on the ground, some were leaping, and others still had sprouted wings and taken flight. The masterpiece didn't show what happened when any of the hopefuls actually reached their goal, but I had a feeling they'd fare no better than Icarus.

As an antechamber to the main event, no doors or side

passages diluted the white room save for the open double doors into the divination chamber, on the opposite wall and the bottom floor. Rugged staircases on the left and right walls led down and widened at the base, mimicking the appearance of the lobby in an old theater. That wasn't too far from the reality, actually. This whole thing was a show.

I started a lap of the balcony to survey the room. Greek statues of flawless marble dotted the second floor, each with its own alcove.

"What do you think?" asked Bernard at my side.

I canted my head. "I think, no matter how big these rooms are, I still get claustrophobic."

That wasn't entirely true. My nervousness stemmed from something more metaphysical than walls. The white room was where Conway had said attendees would have their souls laid bare by the light of God. I wasn't ready for that level of scrutiny.

The gargoyle bristled at the nearest statue.

"Relax," laughed the animist, melting out from what little shadow existed in here. "It's just me." He had squeezed into the small space behind the statue.

I let out a breath, amazed at my relief at seeing him. "Cisco."

"What's the word?"

I made sure no one was coming from the black hall. "I think the Custodian's onto us. He killed the jinn I gave a message to."

He arched an eyebrow. "And he didn't kill you?"

"He needs me."

"To betray him?"

"It's... complicated."

"Okay."

I grimaced. Cisco didn't know my history. That my father had found the ring and had it stolen. That I was a daughter of Solomon. Still, he was voicing a similar concern to my own. It was one thing for Abaddon to need me to power his ring. It was another to actively allow me to work against his interests. What was going on here?

"The Custodian shut the vault doors. Everybody's trapped in the basement."

He grunted. "Including the jinns. That's clever of him."

"Not nearly enough. I discovered a rabbit hole to the Nether. We can escape that way."

"Fat lot of good that does the shah and the scepter."

I opened my mouth to reply but the words caught in my throat. Damn it all. I'd discounted the fact that jinns were barred from entering the Nether. I wasn't even sure if it was physically possible. "Can't they make an exception?"

"Can they? I don't know. But jinns hate everything about the aberrations that live below."

"Ah, so you admit you don't know everything."

"I know one thing for a fact. This shah's arrogant. He's not running to the Nether, not even from an angel. It's not an escape hatch."

"There has to be something," I stressed.

We looked around the room and found ourselves wandering closer to one of the staircases.

"How about a switcheroo?" he asked. "Give him some

fake piece of gold in lieu of the real scepter."

"You've been watching too many heist movies." I shook my head. "Even if we had the time to construct something like that, you're forgetting that Abaddon's an angel. He'll know the difference."

"How? He might be a Celestial but he's from the Pit. He's never seen the scepter."

"I'm not so sure. I'm beginning to think it's a holy symbol. He'd know the difference between a knockoff and the real thing."

Cisco stopped and gripped the balcony railing, visibly frustrated. "Then what?"

I shrugged. "Onward as ever. We'll figure something out."

I set my boot on the cushioned rug of the first step down.

"Shyla!" growled Bernard. "Watch out!"

The gargoyle sprang into action before I saw the burst of light. The painted sun on the ceiling lit up like the real thing. A blur arced toward us. Bernard leapt to intercept the ambush, but all I could make out was an explosion of fire consuming us all.

The Sun of God

It may not have been the light of God purifying my soul, but it was the next best thing. The flames cleared and a man stood near the top of the stairs, bracing the base of a shepherd's crook to Bernard's neck. The gargoyle was on his back like a submissive dog, and the man rested one boot on his exposed chest.

"Hellions," he boomed.

My ASP clicked to full extension and the man's attention swiveled to me. Before he could act, a mass of darkness pounced on him. The staff spun and collided with Cisco's physical form, sending him flying through the air of the first story and back onto the balcony. He slammed into the wall and collapsed close to the statue where I'd found him.

"I know you, black wings," advised the stranger with an authoritative edge. "Do not interfere." His face leveled on me. "I do *not* know you."

I swallowed. The stranger had a wide face, with a mane of dark wavy hair. The scruff of his beard was raw and untrimmed, and his cheeks were weathered by the sun. With a wave of a hand, the heavy double doors of the divination chamber shut by themselves. I guess he wanted privacy.

"Conjurer of devils," he spat, "you are not welcome in this place."

Bernard was sprawled awkwardly with his back on the stairs. His legs were raised defensively, and his stone tail twitched manically. I couldn't for the life of me figure out why he wasn't attempting to escape.

"Let him go," I said.

The shepherd crook pressed into Bernard's neck. "What are you doing here, hellion?"

"It's my fault!" I admitted. "I summoned him. He was just trying to protect me."

But my words had no effect. Instead, he studied my familiar for a long moment. "You were at the Siege of Yeavering Bell."

Bernard's tail pounded the floor again, uncharacteristically perturbed yet well behaved. "I was," he answered.

"You fought alongside the humans."

"I always have."

The stranger lifted the crook and withdrew his foot. Bernard, head low, slunk up the stairs and rounded my legs. I eyed the far wall where Cisco was, but he hadn't stirred. I'd never seen the animist hit so hard before.

"Who are you?" I asked guardedly.

"Take care, human. The questions will be mine. Reveal

your purpose here."

I shifted in place, unsure what to make of this man. Was he an obstacle or an opportunity? I glanced at the painting of the sun on the ceiling, where he had come from, and chewed my lip.

A figure in a cloak strolled across the ground floor. I had no idea where he'd come from, but he walked with purpose and stopped in the center of the room, between the feet of both staircases. The man with the shepherd's crook turned slowly, aware of the new presence, and scoffed. "I'd recognize that stench anywhere."

Asmodeus lowered his hood. "Leave the girl," he said coolly. "She's with me."

The man that must've been an angel completely dismissed my presence to stare down a new rival. "Finally free from Dis," he said with a sneer. "I'm surprised you had the gall to set foot in Creation. Were twenty-and-seven hundred years not lesson enough?"

Another burst of light blinded me. I recoiled as two sets of feathery wings sprouted from the man's back. Asmodeus bit down as the angel took a step into the air and glided down to meet him.

The demon twisted and struck. The angel's staff caught the blow. Asmodeus threw off his cloak and attempted to snag his opponent's crook. The angel tore cloth away and reversed his weapon, slamming Asmodeus to the ground. The demon cried out in pain.

"Fool!" cursed the angel. "You double your trespass with a fight. I am your bane, Asmodeus. I should strike you down where you cower."

I felt a pang of sorrow for the devil, who had a second ago been protecting me. And then I grew angry because of the feeling. Asmodeus was the one who'd stolen the Ring of Solomon and taken my father to Hell. He was the reason my life was a living debt to Abaddon.

And yet, the devil had defended me from the angel.

But I doubted everything was so straightforward. This angel seemed to wield great authority. What if he was the literal answer to my prayers?

"Mercy!" pleaded Asmodeus. "Do not kill me! Not after so long in your prison."

"You earned that prison," returned the angel. "You engineered the fall of Nineveh. And your wicked ways continue. I'll only ask one more time. What are you doing here, devil?"

"I cannot tell you! I cannot say!"

The crook squeezed painfully into his neck. Asmodeus cried out again. And this time, I did truly feel bad. Because I knew he was physically bound from answering by Abaddon's order. By the Ring of Solomon. And I began to wonder if any of this was the demon's free will.

"I was sent by John Conway," I blurted, voice uncertain but bolstered by sheer volume.

I couldn't tell you why that came to me. For some reason, it seemed the right thing to say. Maybe because destroying a portal to Hell was more righteous than stealing a golden scepter. It was something the angel would comprehend.

And it was something that got his attention. His head turned halfway to me, revealing his profile and temporarily halting his prodding staff. "What dealings have you with him?"

I'd been so wrapped up in the moment that I only noticed the Custodian as he walked by me. He paused by my ear and whispered, "Must I do everything myself? Bernard, muzzle her."

The Ring of Solomon glowed and the gargoyle sprang into action. He pulled me from the head of the staircase and put a stony paw over my mouth.

"Whu— Urmph."

But I couldn't speak. Abaddon had commanded my own familiar to act against me.

The Lord of the Pit turned to our guest and grinned from ear to ear. "Azarias!"

The other angel turned in surprise. "Brother?"

"Yes," he said, hopping down the stairs.

Azarias was hit by something close to sentiment. "I haven't seen your countenance in ages, but what is it you're doing here?"

"Tracking one of mine that got loose." Abaddon nodded to Asmodeus. "I'd prefer if you didn't kill him. There are some... politics in Hell he's proven savvy with."

"Oh?" inquired Azarias. He leaned into the demon. "What sort of politics?"

Asmodeus gritted his teeth, but Abaddon gave him a slight nod, allowing him to speak. "Rumblings," said the demon, "about a changing of the guard. Of Hell's Order."

"Is that all?" Azarias seemed unimpressed.

Abaddon nodded along. "It's always the same down there. Exhausting, to be honest."

Azarias grunted in agreement. "You must be careful with this one. He's cleverer than he lets on."

And then Abaddon did something I never thought he'd do. He gave his companion a deferential bow of his head. "Apparently. I won't let it happen again."

I pushed against Bernard, trying to wrangle free, trying to scream. If Abaddon respected Azarias, it was because he was someone who could put a stop to his plans. Someone who could free my father. Azarias was exactly who I needed.

But the gargoyle was too strong. Even my attempts to unsummon him were met with failure. The power of the Ring of Solomon was absolute. I sighed and watched placidly, hoping to allay some of the guilt Bernard must've been feeling.

"I have to say," said Abaddon in reversal, "I'm quite surprised to see you here too, Azarias. I didn't know you lowered yourself to hellion bounties."

"This is a convocation, brother. I cannot allow Creation to suffer when it is most susceptible. And there is something else. An artifact."

"What artifact?"

Azarias shook his head. "It's no matter. Asmodeus has history with some of the jinns in attendance. He probably saw the convocation as an opportunity for a reunion." His staff squeezed the demon's neck. "That will not happen."

Abaddon stepped forward. "Shall I do the honors?"

The angel stepped aside and Abaddon laid his hands on the demon. "Back to Hell with you, where I will personally deal with you later." Asmodeus screamed and winked out.

"What of the others?" asked Azarias.

Bernard pulled me backward as he glanced toward Cisco, and then us. I tried one last time to free myself but was drawn out of view. The angel likely thought we were cowering in his presence.

"Unknowing pawns of the devil," answered Abaddon. "I hope you didn't hurt them?"

"They'll be fine. Just get them out of here. They do not belong."

Abaddon nodded. "Do you need anything else of me?"

"Just stay at hand, brother. We'll speak soon." Azarias spread his wings and leapt straight at the ceiling, disappearing in another blinding flare of white.

Bernard released me. I crawled forward as the light faded, but my hope was gone. Strangely, so was the Custodian. The white room's offer to illuminate my soul had been rescinded. Now it had once again reverted to empty quiet.

At the exit of the black hall and staring over the railing, the Lead stood with her jaw hanging open. She had just learned the truth of it all.

"I'm sorry, Shyla," hurried Bernard. "I couldn't control myself. I—"

I latched my arms around his neck in a hug. "Forget it. Who was that?"

"Azarias?" The gargoyle grunted. "I wish I knew."

I held him fiercely, cursing myself for not having taken action sooner. Azarias was the single being I'd ever met who could put an end to Abaddon's plots, and I had just watched him slip from my grasp.

I pulled away from Bernard and arched an eyebrow. "Yeavering Bell?"

He shrugged a stony shoulder. "It was a smidge before your time."

My phone buzzed.

> **Custodian:** *Proceed with the plan.*

Ceremony

I rounded the balcony back toward the entrance. The Lead's eyes followed me, but she seemed afraid to speak. I continued to where Cisco was groggily lifting his head from the floor.

"You okay?" he asked.

I arched an inquisitive eyebrow. "Me? You're the one on the floor. Impressed with angels yet?"

He snickered and pushed to his knees. "Where's the Custodian?"

I shook my head. "Anywhere. Everywhere."

His expression acknowledged what I already knew. There was little we could do but move forward with the heist, hoping someone or something would stop us.

"How..." started the Lead, finally finding her voice until it cut out. She was unsure how to finish the question.

"You need to forget everything you just saw," I told her. "You're supposed to be at the vault door."

Her lips quivered. "It's locked."

"I'll figure out a way to open it. Even if the Wire's not cooperating."

The Lead let out an exasperated breath. "What's happening to our team?"

"I guess we're not much of one. I never would've thought the one I'd most be sympathizing with was you."

"Ditto."

"Cisco, you still have that burner?"

The animist rose to shaky feet and handed me his phone. It was a fresh one, untraceable by Abaddon. There was no cell signal but it was connected to the internet. I typed in Trap's number and sent him a text. "Got a problem. I'm stuck in the basement of the Conway House. There's a vault door hooked up to the security system. Can you open it without the Wire's cooperation?"

My friend knew it was the night of the heist and must've been glued to his communications. He answered immediately. "Your man had days to prep for this, using a contact inside the security company, and you want me to just go in there and uproot him?"

"Can you do it?"

"It's impossible, and not only a little bit." After a moment, he added to the statement. "But there is one thing I can do. One thing that doesn't take days of expertise to pull off."

"What's that?"

"Set off the alarm. I can trigger their security measures. It should be as easy as pulling a fire alarm. Depending what I flip, it might lock things down or open them up. It's a risk, but it's the best I can offer."

"Set it up." Cisco reached for the phone but I slipped it into my jacket. "I might have something, but it's gonna make a lot of noise. It's an acceptable downside given Cisco and I might be running from an angry contingent of royal jinns." I nodded to the Lead. "Get back to the door. When it opens, be the first one out. Remember to pick up your phone and the pass token so we don't leave anything behind. And slap the Wire for me."

The joke barely drew a smile. She was still in shock, though cogent enough to nod and say, "Got it." I would've been skeptical if her part of the plan involved anything more than running. I wasn't one for pep talks and there wasn't any time, so I left it at that.

"Let's go," I told Cisco, rounding back to the stairway and heading down.

Bernard was already sniffing the doors to the divination chamber as we converged. "It's a full house," he warned.

"See if you can hide in the back. Otherwise you'll need to stay behind." I checked the balcony behind us. The Lead had already disappeared into the black hall.

I pulled the door open a crack and was pleased to find a small antechamber, like in a movie theater. That allowed us to enter without the white room spilling its brightness within. We slipped in to find an audience standing in a semi-circle around an altar. The divination chamber was bowl-shaped and intimate, allowing us to easily look down on the proceedings.

The altar consisted of a marble table and a pentagram

and circle constructed of light-blue gemstone inlaid in the rock. I couldn't identity the material but the workmanship was top notch. It put the custom job in my loft to shame. Ladies and gentlemen, the divinity gate.

Several large chairs sat prominently in the first and lowest row. Most were empty, but the silvans and jinns sat opposite each other. I was used to interacting with demons so I'd expected bizarre, but the figures in attendance were ripped straight from a fairy tale.

The high king of the silvans was a satyr. He was covered in gray fur and had the legs of a horse. On the other side was the shah, a hairless blob of a man, eight-hundred pounds if he was one, lounging on a day bed. His eyes were beady and his ears were pointed and shriveled. The leaders wore formal wraps of green and purple respectively.

"That is all very well," spoke the shah, mid conversation. His voice was pompous and coarse, though it didn't appear the effect was intentional. "Your union is applauded and your heirs noted. As you know, jinns do not engage in such pacts so we can't say congratulations are in order."

The high king smiled tersely. There was no love lost between the two heads of state.

I wandered to one side of the room while Cisco moved to the other. Bernard hugged the back wall. Each king was attended by personal bodyguards, a faun and a minotaur on the silvan side opposite a pair of sand elementals in vaguely Arabian armor. Both sets of guards wore cloaks and, besides their kings, were the only beings present not in their human forms. Since they were all able to use glamours of one fashion or another, this was about a show of status. I recalled Asmodeus and his annoyance with self-important people.

A vertical banner above the altar displayed a phrase in cuneiform symbols. I wasn't sure but assumed the script was Akkadian. I could only translate the name King Sargon. The rest might have referred to him as blessed, or reborn.

"I must confess," announced the silvan king in a more dignified tone, "there is another point of order. These are trying times, and the Nether is not the only domain experiencing upheaval."

"Is that so?" returned the shah derisively. "Under our rule, the Aether is as stable as it's ever been."

"I didn't mean to suggest otherwise. I speak primarily of the World Below, and also of that steppe that spurns us both."

The shah's eyes narrowed. "Earth is not ours."

"No," came a raspy voice from the edge of the room, "but it used to be."

An ancient crone in a black shawl brushed past me from behind. I tensed, ready to defend myself, but she was merely moving to the altar. Two more women, old but not as decrepit, converged from different points in the room. If they had been wearing crimson robes, there was no sign of them now. Their gowns were loose and tattered, with threads worn so thin in places they reminded me of spiderwebs.

Every alarm bell in my body went off. I didn't need to see their gray patchy skin or their pointed black hats to know. These were Cisco's stiges. I tried to find him in the crowd but he was a shadow.

The shah's men moved to surround him, but he waved a lazy finger to call them off. His other hand came into view cradling a golden, jewel-studded scepter in his lap. "This convocation isn't meant for hellions," he said in half-hearted objection.

"And we apologize to the king of kings for the misdirection," said the same woman who first spoke.

Standing in the light beside the others, with their black dresses and torn shawls, they were somewhat interchangeable.

"But there are dealings in the rings of Hell you should be apprised of," added the tallest one.

The third, a heavyset woman, nodded. "We had to choose our allies wisely."

Their inhuman intonations grated the ears.

The shah sighed. "We have no alliance with Stygian witches."

If the massive ruler felt threatened by the devils in his presence, he didn't show it, and, in point of fact, the witches all bowed, deferential to him.

"It is wise to hold off on a decision when one is unwarranted," replied the elder hellion. "I don't need to suggest the wisdom of hearing out a proposition which may bring benefit."

The silvan king receded with his guard now that the witches had the floor. He may have made the introductions, but Vesuvius was no friend of the demons. Had Cisco said they'd been forced into the hellion plot?

Which sounded kind of familiar, and very much the way demons operated.

The shah shared a word with an aide before exhaling. "We will hear you out. But we must warn you in advance. The autonomy of the Aether and jinnkind will not be compromised."

Another bow. "Of course not, your highness. We, as always, leave your domain to you. We merely state our intentions to enter this one."

"You're already breaking Celestial Law by coming here. You mean to make your violation more flagrant."

"There is a Hellwar," said the tall witch. "The laws of the Celestials are an over-complicated framework resting on an over-burdened foundation. They will not stand forever."

"And how does this concern us?" asked the shah defensively.

"It doesn't," returned the witch.

The elder cut in. "We ask merely that you not stand in our way when we reclaim what is ours."

The shah grumbled. "You wish to avoid being cast down again."

Somewhere above, black feathers fluttered and settled. The shah's beady eyes didn't leave the women.

"We can always trade favors," chimed the third witch. "The power of the staff is of great use to us."

The shah's fingers tightened around his scepter.

"It need not be an alliance," she pressed.

"Merely a truce," said another.

Members of the crowd were forced aside as a figure in a

cloak roughly shoved past them.

"Once a witch," growled Cisco, "always a witch."

He leapt over the last row of spectators and landed on one side of the stage, throwing off his cloak. The intimidating effect was lessened due to the faded AC/DC shirt. Still, all eyes in the divination chamber were on him as he smoldered at one witch and then another.

"I've been looking for you..." he snarled.

Fighting Words

The witches of Stygia hissed.

"Vile cretin! You dare intrude here?"

"Vile?" laughed Cisco, pacing with casual confidence but primed for a fight. "You're gonna hurt my feelings, lady. Have you looked in the mirror lately? Pro tip: The 'fairest one of all' doesn't have blotchy gray skin like an overripe corpse. I've raised zombies that look better than you."

They growled in response and huddled together. Spectators turned their heads in private whispers. Bodyguards snapped to defensive positions. I inched closer, keeping my head down, worried that the dumb brute was gonna blow the whole thing.

"Cisco Suarez," enunciated the shah, fingers rapping his golden scepter. Between you and me, he looked more surprised to see Cisco than the stiges, but more evident than that was his disappointed tone. "I thought we made it clear we weren't to cross paths again."

The animist shrugged, keeping his attention on the

witches. "You told me not to go to the Aether, but this time you came to *my* house." Cisco's sneer found the silvan king cowering behind his minotaur. "And don't think *you're* off the hook, Vesuvius. I'm still sour about the whole trying-to-kill-me-for-the-good-of-the-kingdom thing."

The satyr did his best to avoid Cisco's glare and pushed his contingent toward an undignified exit. It seemed that, introductions past, his part in the convocation was complete. The silvans filed out both sets of open doors, and light spilled into the chamber. In the white room, the Custodian and a cloaked figure stood aside to let them pass.

What was it with the angel? He was riding my ass while making us do the heavy lifting. And now he was here, watching our desperate gambit play out. I tried to discreetly catch Cisco's attention to warn him, but he was occupied.

"Where's the one I dealt with before?" he demanded. "I was hoping I could wrap my fingers around her slimy neck again."

The tall witch scowled and advanced. Her hand thrust forward and Cisco jumped to the side as a burst of air lifted his cloak from the floor and swept it away.

Cisco returned the attack with his own brand of spellcraft. Tendrils of shadow lashed forward. The witches in the rear held up defensive palms, protecting the lot of them. The shadows withered from an invisible shield.

"This is no place for battle," snapped the shah.

The lead stige's fingers flared in frustration. She was pissed but deferred to the jinn. Was she that in awe of the staff's power?

The chamber doors swiveled closed. Although the high king had taken a troupe with him, the bulk of the audience remained. Many silvans watched on as their king fled to safety.

With the room newly dark, I could no longer spot the Custodian. I gritted my teeth and nodded to Bernard in the corner. If Abaddon was in here, we had no choice but to steal the scepter. Anything less than successful compliance would end with my head on a pike. I skirted the crowd toward the shah's rear.

"So that's your endgame?" Cisco accused the stiges. "You're bringing the band to Earth?"

"Don't strain your feeble human comprehension with it," snarled the elder witch. "You've spurned Stygia and have very little life left in that bag of bones."

He scoffed and turned to the shah. "They want the scepter, you know."

I froze. The idiot had done it. He'd blown the heist without the smallest fraction of subtlety, and he'd done it in Abaddon's presence. My body flushed with fire at the thought of the angel right behind me. Pure fear kept me from glancing over my shoulder.

The jinn king raised a hairless brow. "The staff is ours, human. There isn't a single being in this underground who can take it from us."

Cisco's gaze paused on me for a split second before passing over. "Well, don't say I didn't warn you."

"He flaunts your authority," spat the heavyset witch.

"Let us deal with him," said the other.

The shah sighed and leaned his chin on a hand, leaving the scepter free in his lap. "Unless it is you who wishes the staff, necromancer? Great humans have held it before." The golden scepter wiggled into the air of its own volition. It rose to the height of his head and hovered between the two of them. "Is that what you think you're destined for? Greatness?"

I moved into position behind the shah's sandmen. The scepter was fifteen feet from me and out in the open.

Cisco stared as the bejeweled relic sparkled. It was right there for the taking. Anyone would've been crazy not to be tempted. I wasn't familiar with Cisco's relationship with the shah, but I knew this had to be a trick. There was no way the jinn would put something of such power up for grabs.

Cisco swallowed at the hunk of gold, then chuckled. "I'm not here for the scepter, I'm here for the witches." He pulled a dagger from his side and slashed the top of his forearm. "I know hellions of your caliber have a penchant for dispelling human magic, but in this steppe, where it was created, how do you fare against human blood?"

He wiped the fluid to his lips and spat a spray of it at them. The witches scattered and hissed, as if Cisco had actually hit on a weakness of hellionkind. I'd never seen anything like it.

Blood was a sacrifice. A binder of contracts. It stood to reason that, wielded in the right hands, it could also be a weapon.

But these witches didn't cower and melt. They sprang into action. Despite their singed flesh, they fired back with an invisible assault. Cisco was battered on one side and then the other. He slipped into the shadow and sidestepped, but the tall witch pulled off her own teleportation trick and appeared at his back. Though she didn't touch him, she bound him in place with open arms.

I watched him struggle before focusing on the shah and then the scepter. Everyone was enthralled by the combat. Maybe they'd heard of Cisco and wanted to see what he could do. Maybe they wanted the stiges to finally take care of him. And, perhaps because Cisco had brazenly defied the shah's request to not fight, he was no longer objecting to combat in the divination chamber.

The golden scepter, the staff, the relic... It idled in the air almost as if forgotten.

Cisco had two witches binding him now, one on each side, magically holding his arms spread open as if he was a puppet on invisible strings. He fought their hold. Waves of black magic roiled across his back. The heavyset witch approached with brandished claws.

"Aw Hell," I muttered. I signaled Bernard to help.

The gargoyle pounced to the stage, mighty wings extended as he nearly blindsided the advancing stige. Instead of being flattened, she vanished. Bernard careened through empty air and hit the marble altar. Chunks of rock broke, none of them Bernard. He turned and growled as the witch reappeared nearby.

"Another hellion flaunting Celestial Law?" she opined.

"No," muttered the elder witch. "This one is not alone."

My ASP swung at the back of her head. Without turning

to look, she lifted her palm and caught the weapon with open air. The baton was frozen, as if it had struck a wall of mud and had become embedded without bouncing. The witch's head swiveled to me.

"Foolish child," she uttered. "Your paltry familiars cannot harm us."

"They're not meant to," snarled Cisco. Partially free from the attention of the stiges, he plunged his blood-covered knife into the witch's side.

"Arghhh!"

She shriveled away from us, knife clattering to the floor. The retreat allowed Cisco to fully break free. He sent a fistful of magic into the tall witch at his side. The blow pushed her back but she kept her feet. Bernard likewise squared off with the third. She vanished and reappeared at will to avoid his strikes.

Which, apparently, was a trick all the stiges could pull off, because I'd lost sight of the elder who'd been stabbed. I found her when dry fingers clamped around my neck from behind.

"I'll kill her," she warned the other combatants.

I ripped the Sigillum Dei from my neck, incanted the first name of God, and shoved it in her face.

The stige's gray mouth warped in agony. She slammed me to the floor and raised both arms. A box of power sprang up around me. It was the same binding Cisco had been fighting against, except it was only one of them and I could barely stand. I used my pentacle to trace an invisible circle of protection around me, unsure if I'd be able to pull it off.

"Enough of this!" boomed Abaddon.

The walls shook. The dark room suddenly brimmed with a fiery glow. The crowd gasped, the stiges spun around in panic, and even the shah rolled to his pitiful feet as the Lord of the Pit descended to the altar.

Divinity

Abaddon's true form resembled the Custodian with notable differences. His chest was broader. His hair wasn't neatly parted and he'd dumped the glasses. His dress was perhaps the starkest change. Abaddon wore a battle suit and skirt of leather, and his eyes burned with miniature suns.

"Be still," he commanded as he stepped into the center of the room. He waved his ringed hand. Bernard lay prostrate and the stiges converged in a defensive huddle.

"Your suggestions fail to compel us," rasped the elder witch.

"Yet I am still Angel of the Abyss."

They growled in response. The angel paced over to me and offered his hand. "Rise, child."

I thought perhaps he was pretending to be a stranger. I played along but refused his help, kicking my boots under me and standing on my own. I dusted my hands on my pants. The Sigillum Dei glowed a faint white, catching the eyes of several.

Although the shah's rotund body was upright, his feet hovered inches from the floor. He made no move to grab his scepter, and his beady eyes hadn't left the angel since he announced himself.

"You're here to enforce Celestial Law," stated one of the witches.

"Am I?" Abaddon studied the trio of black sisters. "We aren't enemies, you and I. In fact, I've already given you a modicum of assistance." The angel nodded toward the exit Vesuvius had fled down. "Not all of the silvan king's subjects are enthusiastic about his cooperation with Stygia. A small resistance tried to get the word out."

"It was you who tipped us off," she realized.

"In service to your own interests," asserted another.

"You can't have the rumblings of Hell reach Earthly ears," added the third.

Abaddon shrugged as if the details were unimportant. "All the more reason to view each other as allies."

The heavyset witch narrowed her yellowing eyes. "Why would you help us?"

"Call it sympathy for the downtrodden."

The angel turned to study Cisco, another "child" of his, but the necromancer met him with a defiant sneer. Abaddon chuckled. "Is it true what he says?" he asked the witches. "Do you want the staff?"

I blinked. Amazingly, Cisco's mention had been so brazen that Abaddon believed it a ruse. And it wasn't a bad one, when you thought about it. Mention the theft. Put the shah on alert. Make him believe the witches are the threat.

And then, when his attention is diverted, take the scepter for ourselves.

"We stated our reasons plain," answered the witch. "Can you claim the same?"

The tall one ground out a chuckle. "We dare not deceive the bearers of hellfire, nor do we wish to."

The third witch snorted. "But the miracles of the staff align with our purposes."

"In more capable hands," pronounced Abaddon, "it can do more to open the doors between worlds than you ever could."

Their conversation gave me shivers. Abaddon was essentially conspiring with Hell.

It was clear he wasn't working with the stiges. In some ways he might've even been competing with them. When it came down to it, though, they weren't going to stand in each other's way. They weren't friends but they weren't enemies.

All the worse for humanity.

"Abaddon," called the shah finally. "We know you not except by name. You should not be here."

The angel turned to the jinn. "Are you presuming to tell me my place?"

"We are not referring to Celestial Law. You do not know this place. Angels shouldn't enter the divination chamber."

A cloaked figure pulled me to the side of the bottom level. "The scepter is unguarded," pointed out Asmodeus. "It is yours."

"Perhaps Abaddon is not a coward," mused the tall witch.

"Perhaps," returned the shah, "he is unaware of what this room is."

I flinched away from Asmodeus but he set a strong arm around my shoulder. "You see a scepter, but it is much more than that. It is the tool of a prophet. A conduit for splitting stone and parting seas."

I blinked uncertainly and met the demon's eyes. "The Staff of Moses."

He showed his teeth. "Of a strong lineage, unseen by human eyes since the destruction of Solomon's Temple by Nebuchadnezzar, king of Babylon."

He nudged me toward the shah. The powerful beings in the room barely noticed the idling of a human. Besides, the stiges were more concerned with Cisco.

"You claim to be a friend," said one of them, "yet this interloper stands in our way into this world."

Another rasped, "We have sworn to see his blood."

Abaddon regarded Cisco with a devilish smile. "And you wish me to withdraw my protection over him?"

The shadow charmer narrowed his eyes. "Maybe I don't need your protection. I can handle these hags on my own."

"Take the staff," urged Asmodeus in a forceful whisper. "Claim your destiny."

I took a step toward the scepter. The witches idled menacingly closer to Cisco. He backtracked nearer the shah, and I saw his plan too late. It was about as dumb and direct as I'd expected of him.

Cisco melted into shadow and slid a few yards, materializing between the shah and his golden relic. The animist snatched it with both hands.

And clapped empty air.

The scepter swirled slightly but remained in place, present but lacking physical form. Which made perfect sense seeing as jinns were immaterial themselves. Fire and air, like the Aether. Logic dictated that there had to be a way to grab it because Ray's summoning marker was purportedly a piece of Maqad, but the theoretical properties of the elemental planes didn't help us in the moment.

I stopped a few feet from it and the shah's gaze flitted to me. I gritted my teeth and waited. Cisco uselessly tried for the scepter a few more times.

"We see," announced the shah, glaring at Cisco's futile attempts, "it is not the Stygian witches who deceive us."

Abaddon tensed. "This was not my intention. The necromancer is no longer under my protection."

The witches cackled. They may have been ancient and decrepit, but they were quick. They lunged, black shawls ruffling with invisible power, claws scraping the air and opening grooves across Cisco's chest.

"You wish to spill your blood?" they taunted.

He recoiled from several blows before wiping his hands with crimson and launching toward them. They scattered from his painful blood magic. More rips opened in his flesh. He cried out and tumbled right beside a docile Bernard, who watched but was unable to assist as long as he was under the charm of the Ring of Solomon.

I abandoned the scepter and stomped over to them, scooping up Cisco's copper knife. As I made for the tall witch, Abaddon clamped my arm in his powerful grip.

"Leave him," he ordered.

I jerked but couldn't overcome his strength. Cisco reeled in pain and the stiges huddled closer to him, licking their lips.

"CEASE THIS AT ONCE!" commanded the shah with the full authority of his station.

The witches snarled and faced him like feeding hyenas wary of a lion. And just like hyenas, it was difficult to tell if they were truly cowed or just biding their time.

"Withdraw," warned the jinn.

"Don't push it," said the elder witch. "We don't answer to you. You don't enforce Celestial Law."

"You're free to open hostilities with jinnkind if you so choose."

They gasped in frustration and pulled away from Cisco. He panted in exhaustion on the floor.

"The necromancer isn't the one who wishes to steal from us," said the ruler. "We know of him, and he is no thief." The shah eyed me sharply as he said this before ultimately facing the angel on my shoulder. "You put them up to this, Abaddon the Destroyer."

He released me. "I'm here to enforce the peace."

"Bang-up job you're doing," coughed Cisco from the floor.

"Don't take us for a fool," pressed the shah. "You desire the staff, yet you cannot have it." He effortlessly whisked it from the air. "This farce is over. The jinns are returning to Maqad. Our protection leaves with us, Cisco, so we advise you follow."

The shah's aides moved for the door, joining a throng of jinn spectators lining up. I hurried over to Cisco and Bernard. I crouched beside the gargoyle and attempted to rouse him from the pacifying effects of the ring.

Abaddon's eyes burned. He lifted a hand and the double doors of the divination chamber flew closed. "It's no use," he boomed. "The underground is sealed. Cut off from the open air, you and your jinns cannot escape."

The shah spun around slowly. "Ah, finally out in the open, are we? It will do you no good, Destroyer." He waved the scepter. "You know as well as we do, the staff cannot be lifted from hallowed hands."

"There's no escape," stressed the angel again, "and *you* know you can only defy me for so long." Abaddon balled his fists into each other.

The shah stared at him for a long moment, and then he sighed. "Then we must take our leave by another means."

Abaddon chuckled. "There are no other means, jinn." He spat the last word like it was bile.

The shah was unimpressed. "That's not a regular circle you're standing on, Destroyer. You still don't know what was built here."

The angel looked down. His boots barely touched the edges of the blue pentagram. He stepped off it in caution, studying the floor for invasive spellcraft.

"And you were right about the witches being deceitful,"

continued the shah, "though it's you they deceive." The ruler nodded to the stiges. "You may proceed with your purpose."

The crones glanced hungrily at each other before forming a circle around the angel. Their fingers tickled the air and the star of blue gemstone lit up like a neon bar sign. Abaddon stumbled forward, almost falling to a knee. The power of the pentagram tugged at him.

"What is this?" he snorted, indignant but intrigued.

The Stygian witches surrounded him, hands reaching toward each other but spaced apart. They chanted in some dead Basque tongue and their feet left the ground. Cisco, seeing the witches with their backs to him, snatched his knife from my hands and crawled toward them.

I held him back. "No."

"It's my chance."

"The angel's worse than them."

"Says you."

I spun him to me. "This is only three of them. You said it yourself, others are missing. Killing one of the witches here won't change anything, but you won't make it out of here alive if Abaddon's free." He shrugged me off with a scowl but didn't argue the point. He knew I was right.

Bernard wobbled closer. "That Ring of Solomon is really doing a number on my head."

"You're back!"

Abaddon continued to struggle against the witches, but it wasn't their power containing him. The divinity gate flushed with bright light, casting the room in a blue glow and painting the walls with moving shadows. The power crawled up a vertical beam of light and collected above the angel's head. An egg-shaped portal opened in the geometric center of the room, floating in the air, as if the bowl shape of the divination chamber was a satellite dish focusing all its power on a single point.

I took out Cisco's phone and messaged Trap. "Whatever you're gonna do, now's the time."

Abaddon's eyes opened wide at the converging power. Despite the portal forming above him, he was being forced downward, toward the hot-blue lines of the pentagram. Whatever magnetic pull it had, it only seemed to affect him.

"Close the portal," he growled.

"Relax, Celestial," said the elder witch in dismissal. "We have no quarrel with you. Hold fast and the divinity gate will let you be."

The shah stepped to Abaddon's side with a rueful grin. "You of all people should know that most of the doors into this world are invisible." He waved his scepter as if making a pronouncement, and then he floated upward and disappeared into the focused blue fire. The shah and the scepter were gone. One by one, his contingent followed.

"No!" cried Abaddon.

He attempted to push to his feet but the gravity was too strong. The divinity gate didn't completely consume, however. It almost seemed content to merely borrow from his power.

I stared in awe at what I was witnessing. I wondered just how much power the portal could take and if it was possible to kill an angel with it. The danger of the portal was clearly why Azarias, the other Celestial, wasn't in here with us.

I'd finally found a weapon against angels.

"You idiot," charged Abaddon to Cisco. "You overplayed our hand, pushed too early, and lost the scepter." He braced his forearm on a knee. "Once I'm free of this I'm going to tear you apart." His head swiveled to me, eyes alight. "I warned you what would happen for losing the scepter. I'm going to smash your gargoyle to dust... I'm going to rend Josalie limb from limb..."

I pulled at Cisco. "We need to get out of here."

"Is that door open yet?" asked Bernard.

"We'll figure it out."

"No," said Cisco. "I can't do that to you."

"You heard Abaddon. We need to leave. Now while the witches are concentrating."

"No. We need to finish the heist." He grabbed my hand as black washed over his shoulders and rolled away like fire. With a force of will, shadowy wings extended from his back. "The shah said this was a door."

I shook my head. "Not for humans. We'll never make it through. We don't even know where it goes."

"Do you trust me?" he asked.

"Not even remotely."

He grabbed me and leapt into the portal.

Fire and Air

Raging hot fire encompassed us. The flames roiled so fast they practically screamed with energy. Cisco's shadow magic, his Wings of Night, kept them at bay the entire transition, but it was no less terrifying. After several seconds of excruciating intensity, we crashed down on the stone floor of a fancy bathhouse, circles of dark magic billowing away from us.

The shah of Maqad hovered before us.

"The High Elemental Plane," I whispered, eyes wide. "It's impossible."

I took in the surroundings. Moorish keyhole arches supported a high ceiling etched with intricate markings. A pool with a raised edge was inlaid into the floor and filled with opaque blue water.

"Not impossible," countered the shah in his coarse tone, "but not entirely welcome. You are now in *our* house, Cisco Suarez."

The animist grimaced in resignation. "It beats being

eviscerated by an angel."

The jinn noted the spattering of black magic clinging to him. "Your wings are impressive, for a human. One day you won't need the assistance of a portal."

"Yeah, well—"

The shah put his hand up and Cisco's mouth disappeared. He tried to object but couldn't make a sound. "Enough of the banter," decreed the shah, focusing on me. "This is about you, isn't it?"

I swallowed. "We came here to warn you. About the scepter."

"And we were warned, but we didn't believe. But there's still more to it than that, isn't there?"

I cleared my throat. "I'm afraid of the consequences of it falling into the wrong hands."

The shah nodded. "Good." He motioned behind me. The golden scepter hovered in the air, gemstones sparkling. "Do you know what it is?"

"The Staff of Moses."

His eyes flared ever so slightly. "A great relic, known for exposing false magic. The staff is famous for transforming to serpents and parting seas and aiding travelers across great spans. But our favorite miracle is much simpler.

"When Moses freed the Israelites from Egypt, they spent many days in the desert. They were thirsty for water where there was none. With the staff, Moses struck a rock and produced a spring. It's a simple thing, really, but the Aether's not a plane of elemental water. As a scarce resource here, the story is meaningful to us."

The ruler took a long breath and stared at something distant. "What your stories don't tell is the fate of the staff. Your people passed it down. Saul, David, Solomon. The relic was closely guarded by the line of kings."

So far that was common knowledge. "It disappeared when Solomon's Temple was destroyed," I finished.

"Disappeared, yes, but not stolen. The Staff of Moses can never be stolen. It's not a carving of wood. It's a blessing; it's a gift." He watched me to make sure I understood before continuing. "When the First Temple was sacked, the staff was given to the jinns who helped build it. It was a promise that our kind would not be enslaved again. The Staff of Moses is a powerful symbol, and not only to humans. Just as it liberated the Israelites, it freed jinnkind as well. And in the Aether it has remained, all these years."

"What does Abaddon want with it?"

The shah cocked his head. "That, we do not know. Jinns are much like humans when it comes to understanding the grand design. But as we told Abaddon, the staff cannot be taken from hallowed hands. Cisco wasn't able to grasp it, and neither would you be."

I traded a glance with the shadow charmer. He'd settled into a silent glare with his arms crossed over his chest. I kind of liked him with no mouth.

The shah leaned forward, toes brushing the stone as he levitated, face close to mine. "But then, you didn't try to steal the staff, did you?"

I involuntarily stepped back. "I..."

He leaned away, perhaps aware of his overbearing

presence. "There are some who have foreseen this moment."

"What moment?"

Twelve sandmen marched into the bathhouse and formed a large circle around us. Cisco flushed with shadow and stepped toward the nearest soldier. The shah pointed his way and he fell over. Two elementals pounced, grabbing him with arms that stretched and curled around his. The sand completely buried his forearms until he was stuck tight.

"What moment?" I asked again.

"A trial," decreed the king of kings, "by fire." His eyes lit up. "Defend yourself!"

I took another backward step but bumped into something hot. I spun, expecting to see the scepter again. Instead a fire giant loomed over me. The thing was pure flame, broiling red in the center with orange wisps for arms. The Sigillum Dei at my neck brightened.

I'd been ambushed before, but I'd never felt so trapped and insignificant as I did below this being. It didn't just radiate power, it thrummed with righteousness. It swung a mighty arm overhead and I could barely leap out of the way. Flames whizzed by, barely searing my hair.

My mind raced but I came up blank. I had no feel for the Intrinsics in this plane. Here I was, a professional summoner, and I couldn't even command a simple elemental in their natural habitat.

"Cisco?" I yelled, backing away from the elemental. "Do something!"

He fought against his captors but couldn't pull free.

With his hands bound, his magic was off the table just like mine was. He was urgently trying to scream but had no mouth.

The fire incarnation punched forward and I dove aside. It wasn't especially quick but I couldn't keep this up forever.

"No," proclaimed the shah. "Do not cower from your destiny, human. To deserve victory, you must first meet it." He leaned forward. "Now, defend yourself!"

I dodged another strike and gritted my teeth. The shah wore a crazed expression on his face. The line of sandmen were perhaps my best hope out of here, and we were hopelessly outnumbered. The fire incarnation stepped into my path. I pulled the Sigillum Dei into my left hand and my ASP into my right.

"Yes," affirmed the shah. "Can you feel it? A changing of the guard."

The elemental charged me. I brandished my pentacle. It glowed brightly but didn't slow the oncoming attack. The fire incarnation lifted a gout of flame high in readiness for an overhead strike. I wavered at the last second.

The amulet wouldn't do anything. It protected against demons. Jinns, elementals, and whatever this was—they weren't of the World Below. I realized I had no hope of countering its magic, its power.

At the same time, I no longer cared. Maybe I was sick of all the bullshit, or maybe I'd been hanging around Cisco too long, but some part of me decided to throw caution to the wind. To Hell with it all. If I was going down, I was going down swinging. The incarnation bore down, waves of heat rushing over my skin, and I swung the ASP as hard as I could to meet the blow.

It was dumb. It was impulsive. I couldn't even tell you what my plan was. But as the fire met my steel baton, it dove inside it. The flames poured forward and vanished into my hand, leaving me holding a molten-red ASP. I screamed but clenched my fist tight. Something told me I couldn't drop it.

"When jinnkind was threatened," said the shah with measured excitement, "the Staff of Moses passed to our hands. Now the humans are once again in need of its miracles, and so it goes to you. Not as a prize, but as a blessing."

My hand shook with incredible pain as my flesh seared. "What are you talking about?"

He splayed his hands to his sides. "Take it, Shyla Crowe. It is a gift from Maqad and all jinnkind. Take it and, perhaps, you can find your own meaning."

Relief flooded my senses as the baton cooled. There was no more fire incarnation, no more threat. The pain receded as the ASP lost its fiery glow. Its weight eased into my grip, flesh cool and renewed.

I blinked at it in awe, and then faced the shah. "I... I don't know what to say."

"Good," he returned. "It is no longer time for talk."

A flash of pure white light engulfed us, and Cisco and I reappeared back in the divination chamber. Only, we arrived just as all Hell was breaking loose.

Hell and High Water

Bernard was the only one who showed interest in our return. He ran over to check on me. Everyone else was in the middle of panic or power. The stiges continued their chant, crescendoing to higher vocal intensities. Abaddon braced against the power sucking him toward the ground. Some spectators ran. Others watched in fascination from the edges of the bowl-shaped room. Most of them were silvans who'd lagged behind, as any jinns should be long gone.

"My mouth's back!" said Cisco excitedly.

Bernard gave him the side-eye.

A rush of power welled in the chamber. Owls in hysterical frenzy flapped in the darkness overhead. The consorts of the witches were eager for the ritual's completion. Black feathers flitted to the floor, the only visible sign of their presence.

An alarm went off. The sound was resonant but distant, originating in the underground lounge or entrance tunnel. I checked the phone. Trap had left a warning message. He'd done it.

"The door's open," I relayed.

Cisco snatched his phone back. "Good. Get out of here."

"Aren't you coming?"

He pulled his knife from his belt. "I've got some witches to take care of."

"Don't be as thickheaded as usual," urged Bernard. "This is our chance to get out clean. With any luck, Abaddon won't be following."

"We can't guarantee that. It doesn't matter anyway. You have what he wants. You got the staff."

With the abrupt chaos, I hadn't noticed the item in my hand. The retracted ASP, only six inches long, dense metal and solid black. It felt heavier somehow. More significant. It was cool to the touch and the palm of my hand was unmarred.

"You pulled off the job," said Cisco. "Your lives are no longer forfeit."

"And what about yours?" I asked.

He shrugged. "I'm not so easy to kill, Shyla. Lots of dead people have tried."

Wings continued flapping overhead. The witches completed their chant and stepped away from the circle. The portal of blue fire winked out, causing the chamber to darken, leaving only faint lines of shrinking blue painting the pentagram. Abaddon, released from the spell, collapsed backward. He rolled to his feet defensively, chest panting and unfortunately not dead.

"There," crooned the elder witch, "you see? You're right

as rain."

He snarled. "I should kill you for using me like that."

The other witches laughed. He glared their way, not noticing as fingers tickled through the bottom of the pentagram, right through the floor as if the stone was an illusion. A slender arm the color of mahogany reached out and around, finding purchase at the solid edge of the pentagram.

"Guys," I chimed. "Am I the only one thinking this is a bad sign?"

The stiges cackled as the form of a female in battle dress climbed out of the pentagram's depths. Though slight in size, she was a mighty figure, with two polearms strapped to her back. A bronze helmet with twisted horns framed a face with sharp cheeks and chin. She was young and beautiful and utterly inhuman. Tan folds of cloth contrasted with her armor and skin, prominently displaying a necklace of light-blue beads and a tunic emblazoned with an eight-pointed star.

"You," said Abaddon flatly as he puffed out his chest.

But the pentagram wasn't done ejecting prisoners. A limp man rolled to the floor, naked and covered in dirt. His ram's head had a long, scruffy beard, with a tongue lolling from his mouth. Another hellion, except this one was dead from a spike driven through his heart.

"Oh crap," I muttered. "I think we just discovered what happened to our missing archons."

"Those?" asked Cisco. "They're hellion kings?"

"The one on the ground is Balam, the deposed king of

Stygia. And the other's our missing queen of Kur. Inanna, the Evening Star. It looks like she was the one who did the deposing."

The goddess rested her foot atop Balam in conquest. The witches cackled and crooned and bowed to their new Stygian archon.

"I am arrived," boomed Inanna, and the entire chamber shook.

At that moment any remaining spectators decided to leave. A mad scramble of cloaks made for the exit. In the ensuing chaos, one figure knelt beside the dead archon and pulled the bloody spike from Balam's chest. Asmodeus rose and met my eyes as he folded it under his cloak.

"Shyla," urged the gargoyle amid the resounding alarm, "the door's open. Let's get out of here."

Another feather fluttered down from the darkness, alabaster amid a snowing of ash. Someone else was entangled with the black owls, and this wasn't Abaddon. I pondered polar opposites and John Conway's comment about being sided with angels. And I remembered the job he was paying me for, although I was beginning to feel the money was inconsequential.

I set my jaw into a sneer. "The divinity gate needs to be destroyed."

"What?" asked my exasperated familiar.

"I said I'd do it. I need to follow through."

I met Cisco's gaze and he returned a firm nod. He wasn't about to run from his fight, and I wouldn't run from mine. We both squared off with the powerful beings on the altar.

"Bernard, at my side."

The last of the spectators had fled, leaving our approach exceedingly obvious. The heavyset stige scowled at Cisco. "You shouldn't have come back here, human."

He scoffed. "You keep saying that word like it's an insult."

"It's a weakness."

She raised clawed fingers and her dress flapped in a blast of unseen force. It was just the back draft. The full force of the magic blistered into Cisco. His black energy coiled away, redirecting the blast without slowing his stride. As he neared, the darkness over his body solidified in pace with his smirk.

Inanna's head turned to him. "Human," she boomed, "you shall kneel at the feet of my children."

The black magic cloaking him rushed away as a hurricane of power twisted him up and into the air. There he froze, suspended, arms and legs thrust outward. It was similar to witch binding, except this power was much more potent. Inanna had barely blinked and Cisco was at her mercy.

Her sharp features pointed my way for the first time. The Sigillum Dei glowed brightly in my hand and I raised the compact staff. A blow of power hit me and slid me backward, but only a few feet. The ASP crackled with protective magic and the Queen of the Night glowered.

Bernard lunged. Inanna swiped a lazy hand in the air and the gargoyle struck the far wall.

"You're one of my subjects," she said with bitterness. "A

child of Kur. Your misplaced loyalty will be punished."

I pushed forward, seeming to gain a foot before being shoved back a few inches. Despite shrugging off the initial blast, a constant wall of force worked against me.

Abaddon stepped forward. "Leave them!" he commanded. His voice didn't have the same resonance, though it carried plenty of weight. His muscles were taut and his eyes burned like holy torches. Even so, he kept his distance from the goddess and the divinity gate.

"Stygia bows not to the Pit of Malebolge," returned Inanna evenly.

"And angels don't fall as easily as hellion archons," he growled in warning. A golden javelin materialized in his grip.

Cisco strained against his binding but could barely manage a wiggle. Bernard was still indestructible, already on his feet and waiting for an opportunity.

"We will have our revenge!" snapped a witch.

"The shadow charmer is ours," agreed another.

Inanna blinked calmly as if a justice at a trial.

Abaddon twisted his lips. "I've offered the necromancer as a show of good faith, but I won't tolerate attacks on those under my purview. That includes the girl."

"And the gargoyle," I insisted. I pushed ahead another few feet but seemed to reach the threshold of my strength. I couldn't approach any closer.

"We're no longer weak pawns," crowed the elder witch. "We're not backing away from this world anymore."

"I'm not asking you to," Abaddon remarked coldly. "Get

out of my way and you'll be more than pleased."

"And if we don't?" asked the third witch.

The double doors of the divination chamber blasted off their hinges. A wash of light flooded over us, and it was more than the spillover of the white room. The angel Azarias brandished his shepherd's crook from the doorway, four feathery wings extended from his back.

"You are not welcome in this world, enchantress."

The angel's voice reverberated just as heavily as the archon's. The stiges cowered from the sound. Inanna faced the new threat, drawing the shorter of two polearms from her back. The handle was like two entwined snakes, and the tip was a large glowing ring.

"Have you ever stopped to wonder, Celestial, who between us was more welcome?"

Azarias waved his crook and the stiges were blown to the back altar. Their black shawls ripped away, revealing horridly uneven skin. Inanna absorbed the impact behind her weapon, but her defense wasn't effortless. I fell forward, no longer subject to the unseen force. Cisco, too, was freed. He crumpled into the viewing stands.

"You're weak here," leveled the Queen of the Night. "We both know this. You dare not approach the divinity gate."

"Your defeat does not require my approach."

"This is not your world anymore," she asserted with a hint of sourness.

"Perhaps," answered the angel, "but it was never yours, enchantress, and never shall it be."

I jumped onto the stage. As Inanna's attention focused on me, Abaddon flared with brilliant fire. Feathered gray wings burst from his back and he sprang forward, pressing the goddess back with his javelin. The stiges hurried to reactivate the portal, but another swipe from the distant shepherd crook toppled them over.

Inanna, though backstepping, hadn't lost her confidence. "You've chosen the wrong side, Abaddon," she spat.

Her eyes flicked over with pure white. The portal blinked to life. Abaddon skidded across the ground toward the pentagram. The light was so bright it seared the stonework.

"With one's power, I shall destroy the other."

Once again, the gate's pull didn't affect anyone but the angels. Azarias shouted from behind me, under obvious strain. "Behold," he cried, "I will stand before you there on the rock." He stepped boldly into the chamber, fighting against losing his footing. "And you shall strike that rock, and water shall come of it!"

I was familiar with the Bible story. It was, perhaps not coincidentally, the personal favorite of the shah's. I drove toward the divinity gate holding the Staff of Moses high. The black metal automatically extended in both directions into a two-foot-long rod and I thrust it down into the center of the pentagram. The ASP slammed into the blue gemstone. A crack broke across the smooth surface. The light of one of the star's lines went out, causing the others to blink and fail. A spiderweb of cracks spread from the initial split, and Inanna shuddered as if she'd been physically struck.

For a moment, time seemed to slow if not stop completely. Everyone in the divination chamber watched the crumbling gate with impending dread. And then a jet of water shot upward, firing a chunk of stone into the air with it.

Bernard whisked me up and toward the doorway, where Cisco was joining us. Azarias stepped past us and approached the breaking dam. The stiges quivered in panic. Inanna sneered at the dead portal. Abaddon waved us away.

"Get out of here!" he ordered with fire in his eyes.

A geyser of water erupted in the center of the stage, obliterating the gemstone circle and overtaking Abaddon and one of the witches. Azarias rushed into the oncoming water as Bernard shoved me out the door.

The white room was empty again, though dimmer than before. A wave burst through behind us as we ran. Instead of rounding up the stairs, Bernard hugged an arm around each of us and launched into the air with spread wings. The mighty leap reached the top balcony as a river of water flooded the bottom floor of the white room. A hairline crack split across the fresco of the sun, and I was starting to think this was gonna result in more than a little water damage. We sprinted into the black hall and didn't stop running.

I wasn't sure where the water was coming from, but the entire mountain must've been filling up. The walls and ground shook with wild tremors as we raced through the halls. Everyone was long gone. The silvans through the rabbit hole, the jinns through the portal, and anyone else with survival instinct through the open doors of the safe.

The volume of the fire alarm overtook the sounds of rushing water as we ascended the stairs into the Conway House. The backyard and house cleared out due to the emergency, with cars collecting at the bottom of the driveway. The Lead had made good on her exit, and our little team of thieves succeeded in a clean getaway.

All things considered.

Battle Lines

The next morning, I strolled up the walkway to John Conway's modest home. The second-story windows were open, taking advantage of the soft breeze. The front door opened before I set foot on the first step.

"This way, Ms. Crowe."

The butler or assistant or whoever he was held the door for me. I glanced at the weathered cross hanging above the threshold. It was stout but old.

"Thank you."

He closed the door behind me as I entered. "Mr. Conway's expecting you in his room."

He pointed up the stairs but didn't make a move for them. I considered interrogating him about his appearance at the convocation but decided it ultimately didn't matter. I continued up on my own. The hall and the room were exactly as they were last time, with all the familiar buzzes and beeps of medical equipment. John set aside an oxygen mask as I entered.

"I brought back your bell," I said, flashing the brass ornament and returning it to the desk I'd found it displayed on.

"A magnitude-5 earthquake," he exclaimed, a hint of respect in his smile. "The basement is flooded where it's not outright destroyed. You drained a third of the mountain reservoir. I suppose you don't do anything without making sure it's done." He chuckled approvingly.

I approached his bedside. "I admit, the plan got away from me a little. The important thing is, the divinity gate is gone. But..."

His features tightened and he nodded slowly. "But you're concerned with what you may have released."

I studied him with curiosity. I wasn't responsible for releasing Inanna, but I did wonder at the ramifications. "You knew about Sargon and the Queen of the Night."

"How could I not?" His jaw ground together. "My father was a great man once, but at some point his only concern was becoming greater. It's why I've adhered to the philosophy of Giving While Living. It serves me better to die broke than rich." He took a long, nostalgic breath. "My mother's death hit my father hard. I don't blame him; it hit me hard too. But I could never forgive him afterward for taking up with that harlot."

The longing in his eyes was obvious. The harlot, I could only assume, was the goddess Inanna herself. Some pantheons held her as a champion of prostitutes and courtesans. Yet I wondered at the significance of Sargon of Akkad, considered responsible for propagating widespread belief in Inanna.

"Your father helped Inanna usurp Balam, didn't he?"

John snorted and continued looking into his past. If I didn't know better, he had purposely ignored the question. "All the biographers will say that my father was a better man than me, that I squandered the family fortune and died in shambles. To me, those things don't preclude greatness. It took me a long time, but I learned holding fast to your principles is what's most important."

I nodded along. It was solid advice, if not somewhat generic. John was in a reminiscing mood, and without anything to add I felt it appropriate to wait him out.

"When you get as old as I am," he said, "looking back with a smile is more important than any supposed greatness." He was lost in his head for a moment until seeming to realize I was there. His focus sharpened on me and he cleared his throat. "My man has your payment, Ms. Crowe. Five hundred thousand dollars in cash. I trust you'll put it to better use than I have."

With his sudden businesslike efficiency, I nodded and inched toward the door, but I couldn't bring myself to leave just yet. John Conway was an aging icon at the end of an interesting life. He wasn't a summoner, but his father had been, which meant he had a rich history rife with occult knowledge. How much did he know that I didn't?

I lingered at the bedside and he cocked his head at me expectantly.

"What you asked before," I murmured, "about being on the side of the angels..."

His curiosity shifted to awe and his eyes widened. "You saw one..."

It wasn't a question but a statement, as if he could see through my eyes into my soul. He suddenly clamped my hand with a firm grip. The old man's body jerked, and he gargled out choking sounds. I opened my mouth to call for help when he rested back against his pillow, his heart rate beeping along normally.

"Are you okay, John?"

The man stretched his neck awkwardly, death grip on my wrist. "You know how humiliating this is?" he rasped. "This dried-out bag of bones is in constant agony." His free hand reached for the controller attached to his IV drip and upped the painkillers. "That's better," he said with a contented sigh.

I jerked my hand free. I knew a demon possession when I saw one. "What's your name?" I demanded, brandishing the Sigillum Dei.

"No need for that, Shyla. You know me as Jackal. With my summoner dead, this is the only way I can visit the Material Plane."

I grew angry at this trespass into a human body. At the blatant disrespect. "Get out of John. You have no right."

"Oh, don't worry. This is only a temporary stop. I haven't visited him before and I won't visit him again. But I can't say the same for others like me..."

My throat caught. He was suggesting John regularly consorted with demons.

"What?" asked Jackal slyly, wearing the old man's cruel

grin. "You didn't think the man was blessed, did you?" He laughed. "John's father made dark deals to amass the family fortune. Instructions were followed and sacrifices were made."

"John Jr. didn't follow in his father's footsteps," I said in defense of the helpless man.

Jackal shrugged. "Maybe not, but the demons have always been around, whispering in his ear. That's why I was so easily able to slip into his skin."

I worked my jaw. Were those whisperers the angels John had thought watched over him? Demons pretending to be angels, angels pretending to be demons—it was enough to give anyone whiplash.

"What are you doing here?" I demanded.

He grinned. "You've inducted yourself into the war."

"What war?"

"The Hellwar, Shyla. You claimed Hell wasn't your business, but you're on the front lines now."

"What are you talking about?"

"The unraveling of Hell's Order. Just as the Queen of the Night stole Kur from her sister thousands of years ago, she now lays claim to Stygia. And there are other changes, many enabled by that bastion of purity you call an angel."

"I'm not Abaddon," I spat.

"He hands you your marching orders, and you return to him with victories in the field. Look at yourself. You're a soldier in his army. And what about your other angel?"

I scrunched my eyebrows. "Azarias? I've never heard of him."

He laughed. "Demons aren't the only ones with many names."

Footsteps rapped the floor behind me. "What are you doing?" cried the butler. He hurried out and returned with a brass incense pail which he wafted over the bedside.

"I... I don't know what happened," I stammered.

"Lucifer calls on you," stressed Jackal. "Lucifer needs you."

I stepped backward under the butler's judgmental glower. John entered a fit of coughing and the heart rate monitor started beeping again, frantically this time. I stood stunned as the incense did its job. John must've been used to it. Fortified against it. He came to and glanced around the room in confusion. I sighed in heavy relief.

"What... How..." His eyes locked on me and he snarled. "YOU!"

I took another step back.

"After I welcomed you into my home!" John's voice rose in timbre until he was yelling. "I thought you were good, but you're evil incarnate. Aren't you? You're no longer welcome in this household, Shyla Crowe. I cast you out! Begone from my sight!"

I tried to explain myself but the old man was raving like a lunatic. His heart rate was spiking like crazy. I stalled, thinking of how I could help.

"Just get out of here!" urged the butler.

I watched them both a second before breaking away. With John rambling incoherently, I raced down the stairs. Jackal was gone. My absence was what John needed the most.

A black medical bag rested at the foot of the staircase. It was open and full of stacks of cash. I counted the bundles and hurried outside. Despite the door being shut, John's accusatory screams escaped the window and followed me all the way to the street, only drowning out under the revving of my motorcycle.

I peeled down the quiet road, wracked with guilt and worry over making a sick man nearly pop a blood vessel. Jackal showed up because of me. That was my fault. Still, the stubborn old man had been surrounded by demons longer than I'd been alive. Cognitive dissonance might never allow him to accept that fact, but I was a constant reminder of it.

Despite all his faults, I still believed John was on the side of good. It took incredible will to fight off his father's demons, even if he hadn't completely succeeded. It took even more determination to slowly give his entire fortune away. I had to believe he could be saved.

Besides, if there was no absolution for people like him, what did that say about people like me?

The Ducati Monster veered down the next street and sped away.

The Short Goodbye

"So you got the staff," said Cisco. He'd stopped by the loft on his way to the airport. "Looks like we'll live to fight another day."

Milena seemed in better spirits. She sat beside Bernard on the floor and gave him a belly rub. I wanted to ask how she was doing, but decided it better not to broach the subject. Happy endings were for fairy tales.

"Fight is right," I said. "There's more going down than I'd imagined. The Ring of Solomon. The Staff of Moses. Azarias, Abaddon, and Inanna." I pressed my lips into a pout. "This is big."

"Uh-huh," he nodded. "It's almost like this town needs someone taking care of it." Cisco watched me expectantly.

I rolled my eyes. "Don't start going preachy on me. It's great when my work aligns with doing the right thing, but charity doesn't pay the bills."

"So this is about a paycheck?"

"Isn't everything?" I sighed, feeling like maybe I'd

pushed my aloofness too far. "I'm sorry I couldn't do more for you."

Milena stood. "Don't worry about it. I've been having on days and off days. I don't think anyone can figure out a way to fix how I feel except for me." She smiled at Cisco and then walked over and gave me a hug. "Thanks for giving me a place to crash."

I shrugged once I was loose. I didn't really know how to handle the touchy-feely crap. Emotion wasn't encouraged in my family, and it was a weakness in my line of work.

"I got the staff," I said, "but you didn't get your stiges."

Cisco cocked his head. "Don't be so sure about that. I know my enemy now. Not just the witches but Inanna too. And while I didn't exactly discover a weakness, I better understand the part hellions play in the order of things, along with angels and jinns. Maybe there's a clue there."

I nodded. "I'll be honest. Even being a summoner, I never figured the shah would command so much respect."

"They're one of three great races created by God, alongside angels and humans." He cleared his throat. "Supposedly. If you believe those things."

I grinned. It was funny how we both dealt with twisted beings of Creation every day, but the existence of God made us uncomfortable. I supposed it was easier to believe in malice. You didn't need to go far in any direction to see it.

"There's a Hellwar," I noted.

"Maybe led by the stiges, maybe not. Either way, they're intent to bring that war to Earth. I don't know why, but those witches are very interested in Miami."

"You think they'll come?"

"I think I'll be ready for them when they do." We shared a solemn gaze.

"What about you?" cut in Milena. "What're you gonna do with your Egyptian cobra?"

I arched an eyebrow. "My what?"

"You know, the famous asp of antiquity?" Milena eyed me and Cisco in disbelief. "Come on, guys. As soon as Cisco told me about the spiritual transference of the staff into the ASP, I made the connection. The Staff of Moses... A staff that transforms to serpents... That ring a bell?"

I forgot how to close my jaw so just let it hang wide.

Cisco snorted in amusement. "She's handy to have around."

I couldn't believe I hadn't made the connection. Then again, the ASP was an old standby of mine. I'd been too close to it to ponder the origin of its name.

And it wasn't anything I had time to digest right now, either. The coincidence was a forceful shove into the concept of fate.

"I don't know," I finally answered. "Abaddon has what he wants, but I'm beginning to question just how instrumental I am in his plans."

Cisco shrugged. "He needed someone unhampered by the divinity gate."

"I suspect it's more than that. As far as I can tell, he wasn't even aware of the gate's presence or danger. Something tells me Abaddon, angel or no, couldn't have retrieved the staff on his own. He needed an operator to accept it as a gift. Maybe it stands to reason that what happens next is my call."

Jackal's accusation that I was already a soldier for Hell made me shudder. Or maybe it was just my buzzing work phone. I received an unencrypted text from the Custodian. A meet, at my place, in an hour.

"So he is still alive," muttered Cisco after I'd shown him the message. "At least he's warning you in advance now."

"He's pleased we completed the job. He'll be even happier when I deliver another month's payment."

The animist wore an odd expression, something close to pity but not as pathetic. "Look at you, making the world a better place and paying for the privilege. Some thief you are."

He meant it as a compliment, but I immediately regretted bringing up my debt. "You guys should probably head out before the Custodian shows up early. It's the cleanest getaway people in this line of work can hope for."

They snickered but took my advice and said their goodbyes. At the door, Cisco mulled me over for a long moment and said, "You be careful, okay?"

"I always am." I patted Bernard on his head.

"If you're ever in Miami," offered Milena, "look us up. The penthouse has an extra bedroom."

"Ooh," said the gargoyle. "I do love a tall building."

"Hey," interrupted Cisco, "she's invited, not you. If it were up to me you'd be staying in a kennel."

Bernard growled and I shut the door.

I took a long breath to center myself. The legwork of our

little score was behind us, but the hard part was yet to come. Instead of relaxing, I dug into my grandmother's grimoire and an old Bible and sat on my bed in study.

Angels and demons were major factions in this mysterious war, and I needed to identify the generals. Of particular note were the newer players to the game, because if there was a Celestial who outranked Abaddon, I could sure use him on my side.

The Bible contained several references to Azarias, and I looked each over. There was the general in the service of Judas Maccabee. There was a man who stood at Ezra's side. Still another was one of three thrown into a fiery furnace. But one Bible story stood out among the rest.

In the deuterocanonical *Book of Tobit*, Tobiah is accompanied on a journey through the desert by Azarias, who protects him and binds a demon. At their destination, he goes on to heal Tobiah's father, Tobit. It is only then that he reveals himself to be the archangel Raphael.

The double set of wings was possible evidence of this theory. If I had any doubt left, the demon Raphael bound in the desert was none other than Asmodeus.

The coincidences were starting to pile up.

Unannounced Guests

I opened the door and the Custodian stepped inside. While I now knew he hadn't perished in the basement flood of the Conway House, I'd at least hoped to see him worse for wear. Instead he was as cool and collected as ever.

Even more surprising was the Lead entering with him.

He caught my confusion as I peeked out the door.

"It's just us. Given the circumstances, I thought it best to discuss events without the Wire."

I shut the door. Despite his polite demeanor, the words sounded ominous.

I couldn't help but wonder, despite his trickery, why an archangel like Raphael would allow him to continue unchecked. But then, Abaddon had put on a good show. At the end there, in the archangel's presence, the Lord of the Pit had been fighting for the good guys. Meanwhile I was left with no way to warn Raphael of the truth.

I led them to the couch. Bernard wasn't with us because I'd had about enough of the Ring of Solomon co-opting his will. Ironically, Abaddon had less power over me if I was alone.

"Where's Cisco?" asked the Custodian nonchalantly.

I shrugged. "Back into the hole he crawled out of, I guess."

It was clear I had no intention of elaborating, and he moved on. "You two were clever back there. Claiming it was the stiges who wanted to steal the scepter. It was reckless and almost backfired, but you came through."

"I said I would."

The Custodian sat on the couch but the Lead stood close like she was waiting for something. With the conversation dead in the water, I looked her over.

"Are you sure you want to be here?" I had a slight edge of warning in my voice that I hoped came off to the Custodian as careless disregard.

"I just wanted to thank you." She clutched my hands eagerly. "You really looked out for me back there."

I swallowed.

The Custodian chuckled from afar. "Did she, though?"

"Don't mention it," I said over him. "It's what a real team does for each other." I started walking her to the door.

The Custodian called from across the room. "The white room shines the truth plain to see, doesn't it? You saw me in my true form, Bethany. Don't think I didn't notice."

She stiffened as the Custodian used her true name. I'd never heard it before, which didn't bode well.

"And you both saw Bedrock for who he is. The demon Asmodeus."

I didn't bother telling him I already knew.

"Unfortunately for you, Bethany, the white room also revealed *your* true form."

She wavered and almost lost her footing. "What do you mean?"

"You betrayed me," he accused.

"N—"

Her voice immediately cut out. She doubled over in a fit of hacking coughs.

I tried to help but something was wrong. "Stop it!" I demanded.

The Custodian spread his hands innocently and folded one leg over the other. I pulled the Lead up and caught her as she collapsed. A croaking gurgle squeezed from her throat. Her eyes locked onto the ceiling and glazed over.

"You okay?" I shook her shoulders. "Hey!"

Asmodeus materialized beside her. The Lead—Bethany—was dead.

"You bastard!"

I lashed out at the demon. My fists pummeled him, but he backed away, unfazed.

"Oh, don't blame him," laughed the Custodian. He waved a hand in the air, displaying the Ring of Solomon. "He works for me, just as you do."

I stopped my emotional attack and stared weakly at the Lead's stiff body.

The Custodian stood and approached us. "There's a lesson here, and I'll tell you what it is. I keep you around because you're useful to me. Bedrock's my assassin, and you are my spy. A summoner with her fingers on the pulse of the various worlds is exceedingly handy during a convocation." He looked down with disdain at the corpse. "Bethany was useful to me too, for a while. And then she decided to go against me so I had to make an example of her. Nice work, Bedrock."

Asmodeus smiled meekly, bowed slightly, and turned to go.

"Not so fast." The angel squared up with the demon and held out an open palm. "The spike, please. I compel you to hand it over."

The demon grinned slyly. "No need. I give it freely." He produced the weapon that had been embedded in Balam's chest and placed it in the angel's hand. It was just a dirty piece of metal.

Abaddon's expression was tickled. "A funny thought occurred to me. You weren't planning on using this against me now, were you?"

Asmodeus bowed. "Of course not, master. I acquired it for your benefit, naturally."

"*Naturally*." The angel examined the spike before stuffing it into a pocket. "You may go now."

Instead of vanishing, the devil proceeded toward my bedroom. I knew what he was going for and beat him to it, if only to stop him from putting his grubby hands on my stuff. I opened the wardrobe and exposed the mirror. Asmodeus walked through the surface and stepped back into Hell. His image winked out and I was suddenly staring at my reflection.

Except a piece of wood peeked out from the inside of my jacket. I reached in and withdrew the Staff of Moses. In my hand it was a small bar of metal, but the reflection revealed it to be several feet long and made of gnarled wood.

"Ah," remarked the Custodian in a pleased voice, "the object of the hour."

If there had been hope of deceiving the Angel of the Abyss, it was now dashed. I almost shoved the ASP back into my jacket, but that would've betrayed weakness. Abaddon was an angel. He knew I had the Staff of Moses. It was better to hold it tight than squirrel it away.

"So all this to acquire the staff," I said. I closed the wardrobe and returned to the living room. "The convocation, an insurrection in Hell, ousting Balam what must've been... fifty years ago?"

He snorted. "You think I had to encourage the hellions to fight and take from each other? No, Shyla, it's survival of the fittest down there. It always has been. It used to be that way with humanity as well. Before the current age, anyway. It made people stronger. Now we're left with pathetic, whimpering populations scared of their own shadows."

His distaste was evident, but so was his honesty. Inanna hadn't taken Stygia at his behest. Once a usurper, always a usurper. Though I had to admit, I'd been so focused on what the hellions wanted to do with Earth that I forgot to consider Abaddon's motives.

"No," he said evenly, "I had nothing to do with Stygia's plots. All I knew was the staff would make an appearance."

"Right, the angelic grapevine." I scowled right back at

him. "Have you ever considered that the rumors of the staff might've come from demons?" I thought of Conway and his whispers. Pretending to be something else was a devil's most effective trick. "Was it possible the stiges used you, the great Destroyer? They leaked the staff's presence to draw you to the divinity gate so they could free their archon."

The Custodian's cheek twitched. He was used to being the one who did the manipulating. Although he must've been smoldering inside, his reply was unemotional. "If that was the case, it was a fair trade."

I didn't believe it for a second.

"Is that what you want, then?" I asked. "The end of the world?"

He scoffed. "You humans are always so focused on the end. What's wrong with beginnings?"

"What's that supposed to mean?"

As he'd done with Asmodeus, Abaddon held an open hand to me. "The staff, please."

I crossed my arms over it protectively. "No compulsion?"

"I can find ways to do so, if I must. Or I can just take it."

"Can you?" I challenged. "Because I have it on good authority this staff can only be given." He clenched his jaw and I strolled close. "Isn't that how this goes? You, an angel, can't take this relic from hallowed hands?"

He smirked. "Hallowed... you?"

"Why not? This was a personal gift from the shah of Maqad. Strange he gave it to me, seeing as he's a jinn and the Ring of Solomon gives you complete control over his race. Did you hold back because of his royal title, or was it because of this?" I wiggled the staff in his face, daring him to take it from me.

Because if he tried, there was absolutely nothing I could do about it.

My eyes never left his, and there was a sparkle of understanding between us.

"It explains so much," I continued, dumbfounded but not showing it. "You never took the Ring of Solomon from my father. You never took it until it was held by a demon. It had been in hallowed hands before that. You're using Hell to do your dirty work."

"A perk of being the Lord of the Pit."

"But a weakness too, because of your rules. The Staff of Moses can counter your authority, can't it?"

Abaddon swallowed his anger and refused to reveal anything. "Give me the staff, Shyla."

"No."

"I won't ask again."

"Then I won't need to repeat my answer."

We squared off for a full minute, nerves taut, faces flushed red. I had better-than-even odds of dying right here and now, but I held my ground just as he held his. Neither of us spoke. We'd already said everything we had to say. And then, surprisingly, the Custodian backed away.

"Shyla, Shyla, Shyla..." he muttered under his breath. He adjusted the wire-frame glasses that softened his glaring gray stare. "You've got it all figured out, haven't you?"

I didn't reply.

"You know what this means, don't you? It means you make the staff your own. Not only have you accepted the gift, but you stake claim to it."

"You better believe it," I growled.

"Good."

He tucked his shirt into his pants and headed for the door.

"Where are you going?" I demanded, following him.

"I'm leaving. We're done here."

"That's it? But what about the staff?"

He spun to me. "What about it? It's rightfully yours, as you say. And you, as my employee, are rightfully mine. Do you think, because you're holding onto a piece of metal, that I get no benefit from it? Look around, Shyla. Everything you see is mine. This loft is mine. Your money is mine. Your father is mine. But closest of all is you." He leaned in, lips inches from mine, stirring my blood. "I'm right here beside you every step of the way." He hiked a shoulder. "And when you're a little slow on the uptake, I can even command Asmodeus to whisper in your ear."

My brow furrowed. "What does Asmodeus have to do with this?"

"It's the reason he went into the Conway House. You aren't the only one who recognizes the utility of demonic whispers. I wanted you to take the Staff of Moses, Shyla, but you had to realize what it was first. When you couldn't figure it out on your own, Asmodeus was there with the necessary revelation at the necessary time. Personally, I expected more from you."

I snorted. I couldn't believe I'd been played so handily. All this time I thought I'd been working against him, but instead I'd given the angel exactly what he wanted.

"Yes," he said with a chuckle after seeing the realization on my face. "I wanted you to have the staff, Shyla, because if you have it, then I have it."

His smug grin turned away as he headed out the door.

"I'll be in touch."

Abaddon, the Custodian, my fucking boss, pompously strode down the hall.

"Sounds like you're screwed," said Josalie, spearing four layers of pancakes onto a fork and swirling them in syrup. "And you're sure you can't just up and quit?"

I sighed. "People in my profession don't have the luxury of calling it quits." I plopped my chin onto my hands, elbows on the table over my uneaten breakfast. This was a hangover even afternoon pancakes couldn't fix.

"By profession, do you mean summoner or thief?"

"Why not both?"

The cafe was properly empty which gave us room to speak freely. Josalie had predicated any meeting of ours to be on neutral territory. This was a public place where she couldn't be ambushed by talking demon statues.

Not to say she didn't trust me. After a few guarded questions, all camaraderie returned. We were like two halves of the Red Sea rushing back together.

Epic metaphors aside, and despite my desire to be an open book, for her safety I kept all developments with biblical ramifications to myself. That meant no mention of the Staff of Moses or the Custodian being an angel-in-disguise. A girl had to keep some secrets.

"What about you?" I asked, feeling we'd been overly focused on my escapades. "You get through that dry spell with Marlon?"

"Dry spell? Honey, we had sex twice this morning. Don't ever let a married couple tell you it's okay to get lazy. I make my man work at it. Otherwise he gets no dessert."

I giggled along with her. "Do I even want to ask what dessert is in this context?"

"Probably not. But speaking of sweets, you're not eating and it's bumming me out." She flagged the waitress down as she was walking past. "Excuse me, my friend's pancakes might be defective. Do you think there's anything you can put on top to make them irresistible?"

The young girl smiled. "Actually, we have a new homemade vanilla bean whipped cream mixed with orange swirl."

Josalie pointed with equal parts determination and amazement. "That. We'll have two sides of that."

"Coming right up."

"Thank you." My best friend turned to me with a

triumphant smile. "Let's see you hold out against that."

I grinned back and picked up my fork and knife in anticipation. It was good to feel normal again, if only for a moment. "You win. Let me tell you, as someone who regularly deals with demons, you drive a hard bargain."

-Finn

If you're reading this, it means you demand more from your urban fantasy. Demons and heists are a riot, but they're nothing without a layered cast of characters and realistic plot drivers. *Summoner For Hire* is my stab at a cut above the rest: non-stop intrigue, true friends banding against impossible odds, and themes that hopefully make you put the book down and ponder, if even for only a minute.

My writing process demands quality control at every step of development. I hope you agree *Summoner For Hire* is the premium product I strive to make it. Unfortunately, doubling down on originality and quality in an on-demand world has drawbacks. It's simply not possible for me to get you a brand-new novel every month or two. The process takes time.

That's where you come in. If you want to be part of building a better book, consider one or all of the following shows of support. The best part? These displays of true fandom don't cost you a penny.

- Join the Outlaw Underground.
  (www.facebook.com/groups/dominofinnfans/)

- Leave an all-too-important review on Amazon. Each one helps more than you know.

- Recommend this book to your buds. Link it on social media.

- Join my reader group newsletter, get a free story, and only hear from me when I have new releases or important news.
  (dominofinn.com/newsletter/)

Simple, right? Five minutes of your time makes a world of difference to me and Shyla. Thank you for your heartfelt support. I'll keep writing as long as you keep reading.

- Domino Finn

Also Try:
Black Magic Outlaw

Did you know Shyla Crowe first appeared in the *Black Magic Outlaw* series?

Did you know she and Cisco share a brief but sordid history?

You absolutely do not need to read *Black Magic Outlaw* to continue your journey with Shyla, but if you want to know his backstory and the details about how they met, you can't beat following along with Cisco too.

And trust me, you're gonna want to see how they met.

Shyla and Bernard have heavyweight roles in Book 4 of the series, but everyone knows the best place to start is the beginning.

Dead Man
Black Magic Outlaw Book One

Also by Domino Finn

SUMMONER FOR HIRE
Tooth and Nail
Hell and High Water

BLACK MAGIC OUTLAW
Dead Man
Shadow Play
Heart Strings
Powder Trade
Fire Water
Death March
Blood Craft

AFTERLIFE ONLINE
Reboot
Black Hat
Trojan
Deadline

SHADE CITY

SYCAMORE MOON
The Seventh Sons
The Blood of Brothers
The Green Children

About the Author

Domino Finn is an award-winning game industry veteran, a media rebel, and a grizzled author of urban fantasy and litRPG. His stories are equal parts spit, beer, and blood, and are notable for treating weighty issues with a supernatural veneer. If Domino has one rallying cry for the world, it's that fantasy is serious business.

Take a stand at _DominoFinn.com_

CPSIA information can be obtained
at www.ICGtesting.com
Printed in the USA
BVHW030230081220
595168BV00011B/435